THORN

By Ian Abdo

ISBN: 0-9864343-1-0
ISBN-13: 978-0-9864343-1-0

Cover Design by Jennifer Davis

Printed in the United States of America

I started this book for myself,
because no one could write it for me.

I finished it for my Jenn.

Prologue

~

Once upon a time in a land far, far away, there lived a black finch. Her full name was Black-Gilded Finch—a cousin of the Black-Rosy Finch as some of you might know. But she found no pleasure in fancy words or frivolous titles. It was one of the few things she preferred to keep simple. Black Finch. Just so. As for the rest: her black plumage suited her nimble shape, with brilliant golden feathers patterning her breast and the inside of her wings (her mother told her to dress more like a lady, to which she always responded, "why?" with all the ebullience of innocence). Her dives were perilous, her loop-de-loops precarious, and her side-to-sides left her friends all crying, "No thank you, Black Finch!" And there wasn't a single trinket, grimcrack, bibelot or bauble she could pass by, as long as it was shiny and she could carry it.

One day, while traveling to visit a boy who had captured her curiosity, she found herself soaring over the chimney forest, a dark and perilous land covered in soot, shuffling tumbles of ash, long shadows, and desolation. She could not climb high enough to mount the mass of black smoke from the thousands of tall, twisted brick stacks below. So, after much struggling and wheezing she shut her eyes, tucked her wings, and twisted downward, plummeting toward the ground like a slow-spiraling knife. Only at the last moment did she open her wings and shoot through the tightly packed chimneys, weaving betwixt warped and wily brick-trunks with ease. The air felt cleaner and cooler near the ground, though not by much. The thickest of the ash fell all around her, floating lazily through the air and collecting in shifting heaps on the ground like fat, gray snowflakes. She knew better than to linger here, where an exceptionally hateful monster roamed.

However, through the haze, a glimmering pile caught the corner of her eye. Something moving. Something silver. With a short, sharp breath, she banked around a chimney, grazing three of its sides with the tip of her wing before descending on her treasure at terrific speed. The haze cleared and she saw the whole scene as she spread her claws and kited her wings for the catch. It was a churning pile of pewter soldiers. They were carrying a small creature of black and gray fur and four flailing limbs, wresting it toward the the gaping mouth of a chimney and the furious and hungry flames within, which cast everything in its seething, wrathful red light.

She swept over the soldiers, snatching up the small creature by its wool, and then beat the air, lunging skyward, fighting desperately to stay aloft as the clatter and chaos of the soldiers faded behind her.

"Old Nick! Old Niiiiiick!" a tiny voice cried out.

Black Finch looked down, and in her strain, saw the creature looking back up at her with its two gawking, bewildered faces, attached to two woolen heads, bouncing about on two different long and slender necks.

"T'aint I," one head said.

"And not me," the other said. "Gift horse and all."

The voice came again, small and shrill. "I will not... be... dissuaded, you duplicitous devil!"

The first head gestured below. "Down there."

"Truth, we've caught a tag-along," the other added.

Black Finch craned her neck to the left and then the right until she caught sight of a pair of pewter legs and the metal base to which they were attached. A soldier had held onto the creature during her rescue. "Let go!" she shouted, watching the gray ground whip by beneath; an awful burning was creeping into her shoulders.

" ... Are you talking to me?" said the Pewter Soldier.

"Yes, you!"

"Never!"

The doll began lurching left and then right. The wool gripped in Black Finch's left foot ripped loose from the doll. She dipped down, plunging her claws in deeper, piercing fabric, and then wrenched everyone to the right. They barely missed the broadside of a chimney.

"That's not us either," the first head wailed, flopping about. "It's the figurine!"

"Pewter Soldier!" the second head corrected with a moan. "Don't make him more cross than he already is!"

Exhausted, caked in soot, and squinting into the thickening downpour, Black Finch couldn't go on any longer. She pitched downward, gliding them toward a deep hill of ash. But the soldier must have swung hard to one side because she was jerked in the opposite direction. Her wing twisted wrong and the three crashed to the ground, rolling and skidding along the hard and torpid soil.

Splayed out on the ground, Black Finch opened her eyes. The pewter soldier was waddling at her, his little pewter musket raised above his head (soldered to his hands), shouting a war-cry in his tireless, tinny voice:

"Taste my mettle, you meddlesome, maleficent maniac!"

With a burst of anger she hopped up and swept her wing like a fan. The soldier tumbled off like a leaf in a gale.

"Doll?" she called out as she jumped to her feet.

"I hope she's not referring to us," she heard one of the heads say.

"We're fine!" the other head called back. "A bit … tangled, but fine!"

Black Finch shook much of the ash from her feathers in a single flurry. Then she hopped toward where she had heard the doll's voices, peering and poking around rocks and dead tufts of grass.

The land hung deathly still. Only the deep and endless mutterings of the fireplaces could be heard, and it was an eternal and pernicious sound.

"What would you prefer to be called?" she asked.

"I would prefer not to be called at all," one of the heads said between grunts and sounds of struggle.

"—Call us grateful if you help us out one more time?" said the other head.

She made her way around the broad and crumbling base of a chimney to find the doll trapped, wedged upside-down between the bricks and a cluster of dead nettle bushes, its four lanky legs peddling the air. Tufts of cotton stuffing were spilling from a tear along its belly.

"You poor dear!" She leaped into the air, hovering above the doll. Taking its back leg in her feet, she pulled it free. It flopped onto the ground with a series of yelps.

"Where is that thing?" the second head said, searching the gray haze as it began to right itself. "The little … man."

She landed and looked about as well. "I do not know. How did you end up out here?"

"—It's a long story."

"—None of your business," they said at the same time.

She eyed the doll as it rose to its feet, steady as a newborn giraffe.

"Well, that's all done," the first head said, motioning to its twin to leave.

"It is not safe out there," Black Finch protested.

"Ah yes, the beastie who stalks this forest? Not one of us is safe."

The second head leaned toward her and whispered, "—But we're on a mission."

"—Dell," the first head interrupted like a warning.

"Oh, right, it's a secret."

"*Dell*!"

The Pewter Soldier broke through the haze, charging at Black Finch once more. "Trickesome scuttle-womp!"

"Thanks for everything!" Dell said as the doll galloped off.

Black Finch threw a worrying glance at the doll before turning on the soldier, her feathers hackled. She opened wide her wings and then threw an even stronger blast of wind at him. But he was ready, diving to the ground and anchoring the butt of his musket deep in the soil as the wild wind charged over him. He sprang to his feet once more.

"You mean little man!" she shouted, and she sent him flying with another gust of wind.

He came for her again.

She rebuffed him.

He tried once more.

Trembling with anger, Black Finch flew high into the air and then dove down, driving him into the soil with her claws, scattering rings of ash and dirt with the impact.

"Now you listen to me—" she began. But she shut her beak when she saw the pewter soldier had covered his face with his musket. He was quietly sobbing.

"That... that is not fair," she stammered.

"Oh, nothing's fair! It's all horrible!" he wailed, and buried his face in his sleeve and sobbed even more loudly.

Black Finch lifted her foot from the soldier's body and hopped from the depression she had made with her landing.

"You were helping them throw that poor doll into the fire. You attacked us—me! You are not allowed to be sad."

"You can't make me *not* feel something!" he said, wiping the pewter tears from his pewter cheeks with his sleeve. "And—and you can't *make* me feel anything while we're at it!"

She ruffled her wings. "I can give you more flying lessons," she said with a glare.

"I'm a coward now!" he said, sitting upright and flopping forward. "Branded! Black-Eyed! Blotted! Eh, besmirched! ..." He sniffled. "... I'm sure there are a few more ..."

"A coward?" She scoffed. "I have a few things I would like to call you, but you are no coward."

"Oh, spare me." he said as he struggled to his feet. "I don't remember throwing down a tin cup." He brushing himself off with short, sharp strokes. But then he froze, his arms and rifle sinking to his sides. "They'll never take me back now."

"Well, you can keep your tragedies and your feelings to yourself!" Black Finch said, and with a flash of her wings she escaped into the thickening ash.

But she didn't go far.

Despite all she had heard of the hateful monster of that chimney forest, she alighted on a shoulder of brick high above the ground and watched the Pewter Soldier.

He stumbled out of the loose dirt, but then sank to his haunches, hunched over and staring listlessly. He sobbed some more. He leaped to his feet and tore up the soil and swatted at the falling ash. Finally, with a deep sigh, he hung his head and trudged away. She followed at a safe distance.

She was surprised by his acute sense of direction. Gliding high above him, masked by the layers of haze, she could still mark with her keen eye where she had crash landed. But the pewter soldier—who should have at least been slightly disoriented—had faced a singular direction and marched forth at a languid pace, directly towards his troop.

Black Finch thought a couple times about the doll as they traveled. She wondered where it had come from, and what its secret mission entailed—truly tantalizing bread crumbs.

—But this soldier is stranger by far.

He stopped abruptly at the edge of a ditch (he seemed to be in such a state that he had not seen it until the last possible moment). To be fair, it was a ditch to Black Finch. To the soldier, it probably looked more like a canyon—or at least the steepest slope down to a black, trickling stream, and an even steeper hill back up the other side. The soldier stood still for a while. Black Finch landed on a chimney, uncertain of how he could traverse it. He turned and walked away. She perked up. At about twenty paces he faced the canyon again, and bent forward in concentration.

You silly thing!

He launched himself forward, waddling faster than she thought was possible. But it wasn't going to be enough. She lean forward. As he approached the edge she leaped from the chimney, flying at him like a bolt of lightning. He threw himself in the air. Black Finch landed behind him, sweeping her wings together. The blast of air carried the soldier across the ditch and sent him skipping along the ground on the opposite side.

By the time he righted himself she had fled back to her perch. He shuffled to the edge of the ditch, shaking his musket over his head, hopping up and down and whooping.

If finches could smile.

He marched on after that with chin held higher. She decided if he was a bundle of cherries he would have a few sweet ones, even though the rest were still hard and bitter.

She could hear her mother's voice in her head, who had a generous amount of opinions about everything, and was always right:

> That little creature is a sink hole.
> Compassion, patience, charity;
> offer it nothing you wish to see again.
>
> *This one is different*, she said to her mother's voice. *This one is trying. Do you not always say that "effort" is the heart of progress?*
>
> (She actually would say "wisdom" is the heart of progress, but Black Finch's mind had already been set.)

Her mother's voice thought it wasn't worthy of a response.

"Not. So. Fast!" a voice boomed.

Black Finch darted for cover. The darkening haze seemed to shift and swirl about them. Even her sharp eye couldn't find where the voice had come from.

The soldier had frozen. He turned about searching hastily, his musket firm in his grip. Five shadows appeared in the haze. They seemed to be approaching the soldier, growing even larger than Black Finch.

The Pewter Soldier stepped toward them. "Who are you? Show yourselves!"

"Not ... So ... Fast!"

The haze parted and five spotted slugs slid into a semi-circle around him, clad in rusted knight's armor and many-plumed helms, their bent and rusted lances pointing down at him.

The Pewter Soldier dug his base into the ground, keeping a stoic watch on all of them.

"A tin man!" the middle one exclaimed from a slovenly, slobbering mouth. The others let out a smattering of chuckles.

"I am made of pewter, sir."

"Oh?" another said, his eyes swiveling at the ends of their stocks. "And I'm made of sweet cream and jelly beans."

"At least his manners aren't—*rusty*," another chimed in, brimming with satisfaction.

"I beg your pardon?" the soldier said with rising ire.

They all howled with laughter, their bodies flopping about freely.

Black Finch twisted the brick beneath her claws. She almost swooped down and snatched out the loudest one's eyes. His joke was not only the worse of the two, but the more dreadfully performed (she should know; she was awful at telling jokes). On top of all of that, there was a time when she relished torturing slugs, a summer she prefers we not discuss. Even so, she found herself salivating.

"Sirs, I will take my leave now."

But the foremost knight barred the soldier's exit with his lance. "I think not, my toy. You see, my compatriots and I have had our fill of jousting this morning. Yes, it's about time for some mild entertainment. Don't you agree, brothers?"

None responded, but they all slithered forward to encircle the Pewter Soldier.

"I warn you now, as gentlemen, you will regret such a fool-hearty act!" he called out as he marched toward them. "You are granted one opportunity to repent."

"Plucky!" one of them exclaimed.

"Tin-acious!" another corrected with a burst of laughter.

Black Finch landed behind the soldier and threw wide her gilded wings. No effort was necessary to appear malevolent.

The slugs howled once more, but now in wretched horror. One tipped over onto his side. They gradually collided with each other, eyes telescoping into their stocks as they attempted to maneuver around each other, to flee, every mollusk for himself. It was the slowest pandemonium she had ever witnessed, though their cries were frenetic. With a flick of her wings, she was gone.

Safe in her perch once more she watched her soldier intently, waiting to see what he would do next. One summer, a long time ago, she would've tied their eye-stocks together into one pustular mass, or perhaps lifted them one by one high into the air, releasing them at the opportune moment over the most opportune pile of rocks (remember, this was a very long time ago)—But the pewter soldier did no such thing. He glanced over his shoulder to find no one, and then looked at the knights with much perplexity as they wailed on—blinded and bumbling, trying in vain to escape from him … apparently. He nodded, and then walked away. She too nodded in approval before taking flight after him.

~

They were drawing near now. Her mind had gathered a ledger of questions she wished she could ask this stalwart soldier: what is his troop going to do to him? Why is he returning? How have they survived the hateful monster of this land for so long? And perhaps the most needling of questions: how do his people endure such asinine beliefs about the nature of courage?

Courage is only part of the whole,
She reiterated to herself—a product of her education,
to map out complex issues:

There are some things rightfully feared, and rightfully avoided. But courage cannot be taught, so … it should be valued, used and refined where it is found.

Black Finch found solace in her own argument. She was often called "reckless and rash" by her mother. In the end, knowing no encouragement could come from anything the voices in her head might offer, she buttoned the futile conversation:

He should be proud of who he is,
And proud of who he is striving to be.

The declaration was as bracing as it was withering. She wondered if she would have the courage to speak to her real mother like that one day.

~

The Pewter Soldier came upon his troop. Black Finch alighted on a thin and twisted branch above them. They were camping near a different ravenous chimney.

"Coward!" a sharp and tinny voice echoed through the wasteland. The soldier glared into his troop, looking for who had spoken.

"Coward!" added another voice.

"Coward! Coward! Coward!"

His waddled steps slowed as the voices mounted, tumbling over each other into a cadence of hateful exprobration. Black Finch shivered on her branch. He stood before them, enduring their wrath for what seemed an eternity. The echos persisted for even longer as they glared at him with silent and iron intolerance.

Say something, she urged him in her heart.

He lifted his head and spoke. "I held onto the doll. I grounded the Aves."

"*Aves!*" someone shouted like a curse.

He shivered, but then continued,"—I could not overcome her. The doll escaped. And so did she."

"Cowardice and failure!" another voice cried. Others joined in, jeering, accusing, despising.

He sank to his knees beneath the volley.

Do not accept this.

"I did all I could," he said, though only one was listening. "I know it was not enough …"

"We would still have the doll if not for you!"

"In our way."

"Holding us back."

"Mucking things up for the rest of us."

Stand up.

Stand up now.

Then, to her astonishment, he did.

"Here come more excuses," a lone voice sneered.

With deliberation, he searched every one of the pewter faces before him, this soldier who had fought the Aves, leaped the chasm, and faced the jousting knights.

"I am not who you make me out to be," he said. "I have claimed my failures. I will not take on yours as well."

"Can't even be grateful we took him back?"

They reared up as one.

"Spoiled bounder waste!"

They beat their muskets against their chests as one, a slow and rhythmic ping of metal on metal.

"To the fire!" one said.

"To the fire!" agreed another.

"To the fire! To the fire!" they screamed as one as they charged at him.

The Pewter Soldier held his ground, readying himself.

Black Finch struck the ground between her soldier and his people. A furious wave of electricity and wind ravaged the troop, scattering them far and wide.

Turning to her soldier, she said, "Come with me, brave one."

It seemed as though he had not heard her. But then he offered her his musket with a vacant expression. In a flurry of feathers she grasped it in her feet and took him from that dark and ashen place.

THORN

Part I

~

1

The young man, dressed in a skirt of black and green spiraled patterns, stood in the field outside the willow grove. He had grown up into a lithe figure; tightly corded muscles, scarred hands and feet, long, knotted hair that fell to his upper back, tied up with a black and golden cord, and keen emerald eyes shadowed by worry. He scratched the garish scar in the nook between his right shoulder and chest, a circuitous symbol of lines and dots. From that scar grew a tangle of Blackroot; it had clawed and woven its way out to grip his whole shoulder as a pauldron, a gnarled, chitinous mass, tough as stone.

The grove lay at the heart of a long and narrow valley, no more than a hundred yards at its greatest width. Steep slopes thriving with tree and shrub rose on either side of this flat lane of grassland, ruddy boulders, and trickling streams. He scratched his scar again, and then wiped his brow. The heat of the late-spring day beat down on him.

Behind him paced a wolf the size of a horse. He knew her sleek fur of black, white, and yellow was bristled. Her fangs were bared. She was a deep rumbling of breath and the soft swish of paws through the grass. He knew, she was glaring at the creature that stood before them:

General Krejcarek loomed over the young man. Broad and round, the general was armored in a spiky, battle-hardened exoskeleton of blood-red plates, sun-bleached and riddled with pockmarks. He had the square head of a termite, with slanted nostril holes just beneath his black, beady eyes, and a ferocious set of mandibles which chewed away ravenously at nothing. His leather harness, belt, and sarouel pants carried many trophies from past conquests; a copper spyglass, a silk handkerchief, a pocket watch and chain, a hanging bundle of shriveled gray monkey paws. A brutish, spiked metal club hung clipped to the side of his belt, swinging like a tail with every motion, and a machete sheathed in leather lay tucked into the front of his belt at a slant. He fingered the handle often, readjusting it compulsively. The young man's eye was drawn to it every time. The more people came to the grove, the more he felt naked compared to their clothing, their lavish armor, and destructive tools.

On the ground lay the peace offering the young man had brought for the General that morning; berries, roots, and a leaf-cone of water, now crushed beneath Krejcarek's steel-toed buckle boots.

Many yards behind the general stood a rank of thirty termite raiders, a pack of restless, wiry scavengers. They had traveled a great distance, now covered in grime and white sand. The young man had had many hours to examine them, removing any doubt about what they had come to do. They carried an assortment of Springfield rifles, axes, machetes, and lumbering equipment; mauls, hooks and ropes, chainsaws; mining hard hats, full-body climbing harnesses, and scraps of leather armor. Some were crouched or sitting in the grass. Some of them leaning against their rusted Triumph 3HWs, or still mounted on their skittish oryx, or the enormous, yawning alligators, weighed down with supplies and metal plating, and all blackened with thick grease and a fine dusting of white sand.

This can only end in a fight.

Still, he had been able to keep the general talking until now—more like insulting, berating, antagonizing—but it was all better than the alternative.

Krejcarek pulled out his pocket watch and sprang open the lid. He squinted his beady eyes at the wolf, one more passing glance. "My men are getting hungry."

The young man shook his head. "There has to be another way."

A tumble of clicks poured out of Krejcarek's mouth, a slovenly chortle. "You are awful at this." He seemed extraordinarily pleased with himself.

The young man resisted wiping his brow.

"He has been patient with you, General," the wolf said through set fangs, the first she had spoken in hours.

Krejcarek snapped the watch closed. "He has shuffled his feet, *dog.*"

The young man clenched his fists.

"Is there no other way?" she said.

Krejcarek stared her down—he had watched her out of the corner of his eye the whole morning. But now he glared openly, his mandibles lifting up like a shivering sneer.

The young man glanced to the wolf, now at his side, crouched low, her lower back raised with fierce and graceful poise.

> *It was always going to end this way.*
> *She knew the whole time.*

He wanted nothing but to wrap his arms around his wolf, to bury his face in her neck, and retreat. This was all he had wanted, since he found her sleeping beneath the grove, since he had awakened her all those years ago. He wanted to be with their family, to hear their daughter's laughter, and their son's endless questions. He wanted to be surrounded by the willows that gave him life, and the guardians that raised him. But he knew his wolf stood beside him for all the same reasons: to protect their family, their children, and their home.

But this is my responsibility.

The young man slid one foot back, tilting his pauldron forward.

I should be able to do this by myself.

Krejcarek placed the watch back into its harness-pocket. "It has been a pleasure to watch you grovel, dog. It's the most I've ever seen from a witch."

Krejcarek spewed venom at the wolf. The young man struck him open-palmed in the body, sending him flying backward and skipping over the grass, all the way back into his rank of rankled soldiers.

The high, sharp crackle of gunfire. Bullets hissed past the young man's head.

The rapid padding of wolf's paws behind him. The young man grabbed hold of her fur as she bolted past, pulling himself onto her back mid-stride. They flew toward the General and his raiders, the grass and soil shredding beneath her claws, a hail of lead and hateful bedlam awaiting them.

He heard the wolf's voice in his head: *On your right.*

He saw it, a raider reloading his rifle while managing the desperate speed of his oryx. Launching himself like an arrow across the battlefield, he tackled the rifleman. He rolled over his head and shoulders, and flung him by the harness into a cluster of distant raiders. They all toppled to the ground. He took a maul from the saddlebag. The oryx caught several bullets as he sprinted away.

The wolf tore through the pack of raiders, her jaws wide, her eyes flashing. Wicked lashes of electricity danced across her fur. Bodies flew, bloodied and spinning into the air. The oryx scattered, wailing. A motorcycle exploded in a heaving blaze of black and red.

The General stood poised near a group of boulders, guarded by four raiders. He was trailing the wolf with a scoped Whitworth rifle.

"Krejcarek!" the young man screamed, sprinting at him. The guards turned. He sent the maul spinning through the air. It glanced off Krejcarek's head. The rifle fired. One of the raiders near the wolf dropped.

Throwing his rifle to the ground, the general twisted like a screw, facing the young man. He threw his arms wide open, shouting, "Come then, boy! Amuse me!"

The young man wove around the first and second guard, dove and scrambled beneath gunfire, and then broke through the final two, gaining momentum as he cast them off. Krejcarek had drawn neither machete nor club.

The young man rammed him at full speed with his pauldron. The dark clap of contact. A crushing, absolute stop. A fist bludgeoned the side of his face. The young man fell, rolling, and then staggered away.

A bullet ricocheted off his pauldron. He ran, barely keeping his feet beneath him. He swung wide of a pickax and then crashed through a couple of bodies, putting distance between himself and the general. His ear was stuffed with searing pain and cotton, maybe even bleeding. Staggering to a halt, he looked back in despair. No one had chased him.

The field lay muddied and burnt, strewn with tools and bodies. Gun fire persisted, an echo of clapping off the slopes. The wolf had sown a winding trail of dead and wounded. Her fur gleamed in the sunlight, slick and matted with blood as she ravaged the raiders with terrifying speed, pausing only to find her next victim. Ten-to-fifteen raiders still remained on their feet, with a couple mounted on their terrified oryx. Some of these were running. Some were circling her, shouting, swinging, and jabbing at her. The young man had only injured a handful, and they had all recovered by now, most likely.

He shook his head.

Not again.

"Phalanx!" Krejcarek's voice rang across the valley, his Whitworth perched on his hip. "Draw the witch to me!" The scattered raiders rushed to him.

The young man scooped up a machete from the charred grass and raced toward the forming rank of raiders. Rifles were reloaded at a fevered pace. Pouches of black powder and mini-ball were poured down the long barrels, ramrods employed, musket caps set, and hammers fully cocked. Every beady eye was fixed on the wolf as she sent the last alligator trundling away, its scales scored and seared.

"Make ready!" Krejcarek said.

The Phalanx staggered their formation.

The young man screamed Krejcarek's name. He approached at an angle, but they could easily turn on him. The wolf twisted about and sped towards the general.

"Take aim!"

Rifles were raised and leveled.

Krejcarek whipped about, training his rifle on the young man.

"Fire!"

The harsh crack of the volley. The lead ball pierced his right arm, wrenching it back and away from his body. The young man half-fell, caught himself, and pushed forward, raising the machete held in his other hand.

"Again!" Krejcarek commanded his rank as he stomped toward the young man, tossing the Whitworth to the ground.

The young man couldn't find the wolf out of the corner of his eye. He focused on the lumbering giant before him. A scream burst from his lips as he swung the machete at the general's face.

Krejcarek slapped the blade from his hand. They collided. Krejcarek wrapped his arms around the young man, trapping him against his chest.

The young man wailed as the air was crushed out of his body. His wounded arm was on fire, his ribs and back strained to the breaking point. He rammed his head into the general's. Disorienting blindness.

"My King sent me to clear this insignificant valley," Krejcarek said, the hairs of his mouth brushing against the young man's cheek, his moist breath reeking of fish and petrol. "The. King. And I do what my King says; but now I'm going to make sure you're alive to watch your home burn to the ground, boy."

A squelching noise. Warm venom struck the side of his face. It burned, chewing away at his flesh.

Everything spun and fell, hitting the ground with a crunch. The growling of the wolf, loud blasts of breath in his ear. Krejcarek grunted.

He squinted an eye open. They were on the ground, the wolf's jaws wrapped around the general's head, shaking it. The venom was still squirting from his nostrils, spitting and oozing over his own face. The wolf's jaws flexed as her lips curled back. The sound of a cracking egg. The young man was free. He crawled away, arm over arm, shaking his head, running the side of his face through the grass to wipe clean the sizzling venom. He glanced over his shoulder more than once. Krejcarek was swaying on one knee, a fist gripping the nape of the wolf's neck. The wolf twisted about, snapping her jaws, trying to wriggle free.

I can't do this.

The phalanx had been shattered, sprawled out on the ground. A few were trying to rise, reaching for any kind of weapon.

He found a lightning-scorched maul, took hold of it, and staggered back.

The two were wrestling on the ground. Krejcarek held the wolf in his vice-like arms, his mandibles locked around her neck as he spewed venom on her face. She twisted about, snapping and snarling, tails of electricity skittering over them. The young man reached the general, planted his feet, and swung the ax in a high arc, driving it deep into the side of his head. The wolf kicked free.

Krejcarek rose slowly, the ax still lodged in his head, now dripping with white blood and steaming venom. The young man looked up at him, sick with dread.

I can't.

Krejcarek rattled the young man's skull with a blow, and then, lifting him above his head, slammed him to the ground with bone-jarring force. A steel-toed boot hammered his stomach, sending him flailing through the air.

His body struck the ground, sliding to a hard stop. He couldn't raise his head. But he saw it, his eye half-closed, peering through the grass:

> The general nodded,
> caught himself,
> and then collapsed.

The last four raiders trained their rifles on the wolf.

> She hedged them away from the grove,
> her body arched, electricity dancing over her fur,
> scouring the grass at her feet.

They heaved Krejcarek's limp body onto an oryx.

> They rode away,
> their rifles still aimed back at the wolf.

Ian Abdo

2

"I have to leave today."

"Why?"

He felt grass between his fingers. Different. Smooth. Warmed by the sun. He was in some sort of field.

"There's a lemur nearby. She's my guide. She says I have to leave."

The old witch is here?
Who's talking?

"Why must you leave?"

"Because she told me so."

"Because she told you so?"

He was holding onto a silver pendant hanging from his neck.

When did she give me her pendant?

A young girl walked to him on her knees. She wore a sheer summer dress, her strawberry-blonde hair gathered back and held up with gilded pins. Inquisitive eyes and a pixie smile. She lifted her dress as she crawled onto him and sat in his lap (he was sitting, he realized). Her face next to his, looking him over with quiet satisfaction. Silk and flesh, grass and wildflowers. The sweat on his skin. All the sensations swelled up, filling him, overwhelming him.

"You are welcome here. You may come and go as you please." Her breath smelled of blueberries and ginger.

I remember this.

A second girl sidled up behind him, her breasts pressed against his back, her thighs clutching his hips. "You can say it."

"I am welcome here. I can come and go as I please." He heard the words come out of his mouth, but it wasn't his mouth, and the voice was the voice of a boy.

He leaned into the first girl, his lips pursed. She arched back out of reach.

This is a dream.

"Stay with us," the second girl said as her fingers played along the nape of his neck, pulling at the short hairs.

A third girl leaned against his arm, softly kissing his shoulder. "Stay with us."

The heat of flesh; the scent of hair; silk surrounded him, caressing him, holding him. His heartbeat pounded in his ears. One hand rested on warm skin, the other gripping silk. His small hand, the hand of a child. The meadow awakened around him: the tall, tumbling green grass, the golden morning light, the robust wall of oaks that encircled them.

"You are welcome here," the first girl said.

Don't say it.
Just leave.

She put her hands behind her head, in her hair, pulling out the pins. She blocked out the sun. He blinked.

"I want to stay," he heard the boy say with his mouth.

The girl let down her hair. It tumbled like golden rivers over her shoulders, down her chest and onto him before pouring over the meadow, roiling, sweeping out into the coming shadows. The young man braced himself.

She leaned in.

The wind died.

The young man recoiled, but the boy looked up with such awe, just like he remembered doing, so many years ago.

Round lips, dark as blood.

A wondrous shock, like succulent thorn-pricks.

The world fell to black.

But he jerked back as he slipped, sliding, and then falling down into the void. There was nothing to hold onto. Its strength was ravenous. He strained, stretching until he thought he would tear, reaching out for the horizon of dimming light. It dragged him down, down, down. With a burst of frantic strength, he wriggled his way up. It clawed desperately at his legs with every gain, pulling flesh from bone, wrenching bone from socket. With a twist and a lurch he fell to the grass, rolled away, and scrambled to a safe distance. He was in his own body once more. He slumping to the ground.

Staring through blades of grass, he watched the first girl dragging the boy away by his arm. The other two followed close behind. He pushed himself from the ground, caught up to them with a hobbled jog, and then fell into pace at the end of their grave procession, listening and watching.

The young man had explored innumerable dreams through the years, ever since he first left the grove— dreams of distant places and times and every sort of people. He had grown accustomed in navigating these nightly curiosities, teasing out the peculiar way of each adventure, sometimes even reveling in them.

But here, in this meadow, following these girls, he felt something in the cooling air that clutched his skin, something in his feet as they pressed the warm grass to the ground, one foot after the other. He could see it in the heavy, heavy sky above. And as the color seeped away leaving only night, it left a stark truth that he understood without a doubt:

This isn't a dream.

He scratched his scar.

They had almost reached the edge of the meadow. The third girl wrapped her arms around her waist; her pace slowed. "It will not be enough."

"Ymrosch will keep his word," the second girl said, her chin high.

The first girl stopped and spun about with wild hair and willful eyes. "*Ymrosch—*" she said, her lips twisted in disgust, "—will do what he must. So will we." She turned back and continued her uneven march, pulling the boy along behind her, the grass hissing as his limp body flattened a narrow lane through it.

The third girl watched them take him away. "I wish it didn't have to be him," she whispered. Hurrying to catch up, she passed the second girl and took hold of the boy's legs, working to lift him from the ground. The second girl sighed and then reluctantly joined in, grabbing his dangling arm and then taking the one her sister held.

"Fine," the first girl said and strode ahead of her sisters, leading the way into the shadowed oaks.

"She'll be careful," the second girl assured the third one, smiling despite her awkward gait. "He won't miss it when it's gone."

The young man kept close to them, a frown on his face.

Following them, he found himself in a secluded hollow, surrounded by seven low-burning torches. At its center was the soft nest of leaves where he had slept many years ago, when he had been the foolish boy he saw unconscious before him. He looked around the hollow warily.

The two girls laid the boy gently onto the nest, setting his legs straight and his hands at his sides before standing, one on either side of him. The first girl had been wandering the hollow, breathing deep and hissing, her eyes closed, her long, wild hair trailing behind her. At last, positioning herself at the head of the nest, she glared at the young man. He bent down, staring back at her. The hair on his arms rose.

She clapped her hands twice. The ground thrummed and swelled beneath his feet. The torches pitched, slanting hard in different directions. Some swung about in slow circles. In a single, arduous eruption they rose from where they were planted. But what broke free, burrowing out of the solid earth, were seven enormous creatures.

The young man staggered away in the upheaval, hiding among the oaks—but not too far, unwilling to leave his young self alone with them. Round as turnips, massive as boulders, they righted themselves. Soil, root, and dead leaf shed from their deep brown coats of thick, thick stubble. The torches, now high above, cast heavy shadow from atop these creatures who creaked and groaned like old boughs as they settled, shifting back and forth on their countless, wretched and root-like legs. The young man maneuvered about, barely able to see between them. His scar itched. He scratched at it.

When they all stood at attention, the first girl lifted her voice. "Find his companion. Entertain her."

Four of the creatures scuttled out of the hollow, one after the other, taking their light with them. The three remaining creatures stationed themselves evenly around the edge of the hollow.

The young man crept forward. The only sound was the dry crackle of the torches. Their meager light sent many shifting shadows dancing around the hollow, stretching their long and restless forms. Everything glimmered in the orange hue, obscured by the fickle darkness; here a demure smile, there an unfurling claw; here a coil of strawberry-blonde hair, there a sweeping, serpentine tail. He crouched behind one of the creatures, where he could keep watch; a chill emanated from its great body, and its dank, humid odor filled his nostrils.

A voice rose, thin and timid, a quivering tone that floated through the stagnant air: the third girl began to sing from the far-edge of the circle, a small, slender silhouette between the giant torch creatures:

Hush now, little one,
Hush now.
The day is done and time has come
to lay your sweet head down.
Hush now, little one,
Hush now.
I've swept all trouble far from here,
to ease your troubled brow.

The second girl took to her knees beside the nest, digging a small hole with both hands, her body bent forward to begin the next scoop. The first girl held something high above her head. It was long, smooth and gleaming, and curved like a horn, like a giant fang, like a pale stone. She stabbed at her forearm in a frenzied burst. When the light found her again her slender arm, splattered with black blood, hung extended over the finished hole. Glistening streams poured down, a pattering of noises as it struck the ground.

His scar itched. He flexed his shoulder.

The second girl, her fair skin now smeared with dirt, slouched out of her dress, dropping it into the hole of pooling liquid. She left it there and crawled toward the young man, one claw outstretched, and then the next. Then she was seated near him, between the torch giants, facing in with legs crossed, elbows out and her hands on her thighs, head hung low and covered by drapes of dirt-caked hair. He was close enough to see the sharp ridges of her scaled spine, bowed forward, undulating with every urgent breath.

Slap, slap, slap!

She clapped her palms against her inner thighs. Two beats of silence, then she began again.

She struck herself with fury, her head and hair shaking from the height she lifted her arms and the strength with which she brought them down. She was keeping rhythm for her sister's tremulous lullaby.

His scar burned. He dug his fingers into it, tugging at it, feeling it grip his chest in resistance.

The first girl held aloft her sister's darkly-drenched dress, a leaden, sopping mess, and then draped it over the boy's wrist, over the willow bracelet. Three times she wrapped it round, and tied it firmly with a squelching noise.

He shook his head.

He grit his teeth.

This already happened.

Even so he inched forward, steeling himself to rescue the boy.

The torch creature shuddered as a deep, deep groan seized the hollow. The young man toppled back, covering his ears. He rolled onto his side and pressed his forehead to the ground, his eyes shut from pain. His whole body trembled from the sound, and his heart felt like it couldn't keep beating beneath such oppression.

He wanted to run.

But he couldn't leave the boy behind.

Hush now, little one,
Hush now.

He saw the first girl at the head of the nest, the darkly-spattered horn lifted high above her head once more. Her outstretched arm gleamed, covered in dark scales. Her tail curled and whipped behind her. She was whispering something he couldn't hear, her fangs shining, her round lips taking a different shape every time the light hit them, her eyes empty as pits.

Slap, slap, slap!

The young man staggered to his feet, his head spinning. He tore at his searing scar, ripping pieces free, the sensation slicing through him with every tangled fistful.

This already happened.

"Stay away from him!" the young man shouted, charging at her, though he was moving backwards.

The girl drove the horn into the boy's belly.

The young man collapsed to his knees. A horrific gap opened in his stomach.

The boy awoke. He thrashed about like a pinned insect, his shrieking barely audible over the pandemonium.

> Hush now, little one,
> Hush now.

The young man retched blood. He dropped to the ground. Thousands of roots burst from his scar, skittering down his body, needling deep into the soil, binding him, choking him, pulling him in. The ground swallowed his body in its cold and absolute embrace. Damp soil crawled into his mouth.

Something was being drawn out of him—something out of the boy.

A brilliant green light; blinding, nauseating.

He shook his head, his whole body trembling, straining for one, last, look.

She drew a shining blade from the boy.

~

The young man burst to frantic life. A hand rested gently on his scar. Every muscle released at the familiar touch.

"They are gone."

His eyes focused. The wolf had changed back into her true form: the young witch crouched over him, sniffing at him, her hands examining him thoroughly.

Fair skin, short and wild black hair, black eyes ringed in gold, a black dress and cloth gauntlets, and much gilded jewelry; many rings, earrings, a lip ring, and bracelets. She was always nice to look at her. White and crimson blood and black soil covered her whole body. Concern strained her filthy, lovely face—an expression he knew well. It caused the tear-like scar beside her eye to pucker.

He smiled, a little sweet, a little bitter. "Are you okay?"

"Of course," she said, wiping the blood from her mouth, smearing it across her makeup.

Of course.

"How long was I—?"

"A few moments," she said, before glancing over her shoulder, toward the entrance of the valley. He lifted his head. The surviving raiders were a speck on the horizon, retreating. He laid back down with a grunt. His arm throbbed with pain. The rest of him ached horribly.

"You had another one," she said as she rummaged through her leather belt of pouches and satchels.

"I'm fine."

"It was bad."

"It was … different."

"We should talk with Tiger." She pulled out the bundled strips of cloth and smaller bags of salves and powders and laid them on the young man's stomach.

He squinted up into the afternoon sky, his vision swimming. He laid his good arm over his eyes. "Okay, this evening."

3

The young man leaned on the witch as they hobbled into the curtains of willow branches. The light inside was stark. Long fans of leaves brushed against his skin. He parted the branches with his good arm. They didn't embrace him like they had when he was a boy. The earthen smell of living bark and foliage filled his nostrils, but it was not as pungent as before. He had accepted the way the willows had changed toward him. They had watched him, time after time, go out to try and protect them from vicious animals, thieves, and raiders —and watched him fail again, and again, and again. He knew how they looked down on him now: dazed, battered, burned, his arm in a sling, nursing cracked ribs, covered in cuts and bruises and bandages.

In many ways the distance he felt was a relief. And even if that wasn't entirely true, what good comes from missing something that can never be recovered? He knew all of these thoughts and feelings had been uprooted because of his vision, seeing the innocent child he used to be, remembering all he had lost—and perhaps even something he never knew had been taken.

We will figure this out, the witch thought, her heart reaching out to his.

Realizing how far he had strayed into his thoughts, he hugged her with the arm hanging around her shoulders.

Sorry.
She narrowed her gaze. *What do we say?*

He couldn't resist smiling. With a chuckle he said aloud, "I'm not sorry."

A curt nod. She almost smiled in her dry, subtle way. "It is the concussion. Remember to breathe, and move slowly. We should get you some water as well."

"Hey now, this isn't my first head wound."

"Yeah, yeah."

The two stepped out of the willow branches and into the grove. Vibrant colors teemed from the brilliant green leaves, the rich, red bark, and the rainbow of rampant, wondrous wildflowers. White and feathery pollen swam in the air. Gentle rains kissed the lush foliage, and shafts of gilded sunlight poured through the canopy. In all of his adventures he had never found another place like it.

He stopped and looked to his right, spying a tuft of mousy brown hair hidden among the brush. But he knew what he would find before he looked.

"You were supposed to stay with Tiger," he said.

The tuft of hair shifted, stilled, and then emerged. A girl, plump yet sprightly, rushed out of the bushes and then stumbled to a stop before them, her hands clasped behind her back, her shoulders lifted, and her face downcast.

"I ... I wanted to see you," she said.

The young man tried to remain stoic; her mess of long and knotted hair; her dirt-smudged face.

She is every bit your daughter, the witch thought, a deft expression of both adoration and resignation.

And yet, there was too much of her mother in her to be ignored, beyond the girl's wily, irksome willfulness. There was her fashion: a skirt of black with a brown spiral pattern (which she had chosen), a matching top, and the way she tied back her hair, a fastidious display of loops and ties (which no one had taught her). And, of course, there were her eyes: black, and ringed with gold. The young man never stood a chance.

I should sit and talk with her, he thought.
The witch patted him softly on the stomach. —*And no one is surprised.*

"Kiss your mother," he said aloud.
The young witch bent down, having washed most of the battleground from her face. The girl hopped to her mother, rose on tip-toes, and kissed her on the cheek.
"Thank you, sweet pea," the witch said. "I will call the guardians. Do not take too long." Then she left the two alone in the clearing.
He sat down on the fallen log with a grunt. The girl crawled up next to him. They stared into the archway, watching the willow branches sway, and the shafts of emerald light that pierced the restless, floral veil. His cuts and bruises ached. The side of his face felt numb, where it didn't feel on fire. Exhaustion radiated from his skin like a fever, and all the more seated next to his energetic daughter.

Ian Abdo

She injured herself a fair amount. He had watched her fall from trees, trip over rocks, and get scratched and bruised from playing with the animals (especially Tiger, who, he was fairly certain was already training her), but she always hopped back up and kept going. There may have been tears, and sometimes she still ran to his arms, but all things mended quickly for her. She had no idea what it felt like to be weary.

Weariness and hunger,
doubt and fear...

Her hair brushed his shoulder and he raised his good arm with a grunt, letting her scoot close, resting her head gently against his bandaged chest. He wrapped his arm around her with a sigh. His small, sweet person. She used to be so much smaller. He remembered when she was a bundle of soft fabric and fragile flesh which he held tucked beneath his arm as he wandered about the grove, to soothe her, quiet her—and perhaps, on a particularly lucky night—even lull her to sleep. But every day she was changing, growing, and becoming more and more like her mother—her mother, who ran away from home as a child. A heart-withering thought.

"You got hurt," she said.

"Yeah, they got me good."

"But you beat them?"

He almost answered, paused, and then said, "No, it was your mother. Her wolf sent them all running scared."

She picked at his skirt. "But you scared them too, right?"

"A couple of them. Maybe."

His daughter sat very still, her hand resting on his leg. She had another question for him, he could feel the tension in her. He already knew the question because he had answered it many times before.

" ... What was the sky like?" she asked.

He pressed his lips to her head as he searched in vain for a new way to say it. But there wasn't.

"It was blue."

"Were there clouds?"

"Yes, some soft clouds. But it was mostly clear."

"And the sun?" she added without pause.

"It was shining."

Her body slumped into his, a heavy weight of longing.

"But it's not always like that," he said, reminding her, one more time; "Sometimes the sun burns very, very hot. Sometimes the sky is one giant sheet of white, and all you feel is the bite of ... of winter's white teeth." The words had come out of his mouth before he realized it.

He should've started talking to her about these things when she first asked, a few years ago. He didn't know why he loathed the idea. He wanted to explain it better than the old witch. He just wished he didn't have to do it now.

"There is a big world out there," he said, measuring out each word. "And there are lots of beautiful things, but there are bad things too, dangerous things. And yes, there are people out there, but some of them are terrifying. Some lie to you, try and hurt you, try and take things from you ..." He drew in a turbulent breath. "No one out there will look out for you like we do. And they will never take care of you the way we take care of each other."

She nodded.

He couldn't tell if she felt safe or despondent.

The old witch did it better.

She was picking at a loose thread in his skirt. Round little hands with strong fingers. Plenty of dirt beneath the nails, and a bracelet of living willow bark around her wrist. He didn't know why he hadn't seen it before. His neck flushed with heat. Maybe his concussion was worse than he thought.

He reached for it, but then recoiled, groaning from the bullet wound.

"Are you okay?" she said, sitting up.

"Where did you get that bracelet?"

"The willows gave it to me."

"When? When did they give it to you?"

"Last night, when I was sleeping. When did they give you your bracelet?"

He reached out, grabbing hold of his daughter's hand. He looked up, searching the high canopy, knowing his urgent questions would never be answered. The branches bowed and shifted with ease. The leaves shivered in the wind, their many sounds like scattered whispers overhead. He rose to his feet, standing between his daughter and the archway of willows.

"What do we do if we're scared?" he demanded, turning on her.

His daughter's body tensed.

"If you see fire, if you hear bad noises?" he added, his voice growing louder.

"To the circle," she whispered, her head tucked to her chest.

He gripped her hand, pulling it toward himself. "Speak up."

"Run to the circle."

"—And find Tiger," he prompted. "Say all of it."

"I don't want to," she quaked.

"This is important," he urged, bending down to meet her, face to face. "Say it."

She leaned away, trying to pull her hand free. "I don't want to do this, please!"

"I need to hear you say it!" he shouted.

"You're hurting me!" The girl cried.

He let go. She cradled her hand in her lap, sitting fearfully still. He could've crushed her bones without realizing it. But he hadn't. There was no comfort in that.

The longest silence.

He needed her to be safe. Couldn't she see that? If she just said the words. That's all he needed. And now he had hurt his girl. He opened his mouth to speak several times but the right thing to say was never there.

She's going to remember this moment.

"I'm sorry," he said. "Did I hurt you? I'm so sorry."

"It's okay," she said, looking up at him with tear-filled eyes.

"I'm so sorry." He wrapped his arms around her.

She pressed into him as though he was rescuing her. He held her with a desperate yet controlled strength. His chest and arm burned from his wounds. His breath trembled, his body bent beneath the strain, but he refused to let her go. His fears would wait. He could endure his own helplessness later. He was going to hold her until she let go, no matter how painful it became.

Ian Abdo

4

At the heart of the grove stood a circle of ancient willows. Their thick roots radiated across the grassy clearing, weaving their intricate patterns before slipping beneath the soil. Each trunk was unique, some thinner and slightly leaning, others hefty and twisted, yet they were all grand in their silent vigil. The greatest willow towered over the others, rich with nooks and hollows, old and brutal scars, wild, prolific shoots, moss, and flowers, and thick, spiraling boughs, which wove back into the broad and sinuous tree many times before reaching out, spreading their foliage over the clearing. Long, pendulous branches played with the shafts of evening's light and the clouds of silver pollen.

Opposite the great willow sat the stone dais of the guardians; it was a broad and many-tiered slab of stone which jutted into the circle from between two willows.

At the very center of it all grew the cradle-flower from which the young man had been born, its dense stock bowed forward, its delicate fans of flesh-colored petals unfurled. Its sepals had just begun to curl up, composed for the coming of night.

When they had gathered, he told his vision to Tiger, Python, Monkey, and the young witch. He stood before his three giant guardians seated on their stone dais. The young witch sat to the side. He took his time to make sure he had not forgotten any detail. The only thing he did not share was how the boy had awakened during the ceremony.

Tiger sat foremost on the dais, his massive paws crossed, his glowing, amber eyes half-closed, and his many tails switching back and forth from time to time. His silken coat shone in the evening lights, black fur with purple stripes—in the traditional pattern, he was fond of reminding them. Despite his indolent airs, the young man knew Tiger's whole attention was fixed on him, already parceling out the facts of the vision with his tactical mind. Tiger's training had become more difficult over the past few years. The young man felt he could do nothing to please him. He was eager to hear Tiger's opinion.

Python must have coiled up on the tallest pedestal of stone, to the left, her head swaying high above. The young man had to guess because she had made her scales so dark that he couldn't see her, and she sat as silent as the stones themselves. Python always preferred the high ground because she liked to see everything, learn everything she possibly could. She was taking in his whole story, he knew, letting it filter through her contemplative, exacting intellect.

Monkey was doing a head-stand, his gangly legs and long tails wagging in the air to keep balance. At the beginning of the young man's story he had been sitting cross-legged, his brow well-and-furrowed, methodically picking at his bristled, rust-colored fur, and casting away whatever he found with stoic resolution. But then he laid on his belly, both hands propping up his chin. At one point he flopped onto his back with a leg hanging off the dais. But he ended up on his head, a pink tongue stuck out in concentration. Monkey's thoughts were forever a mystery; or maybe he chose not to think at all? The young man loved him for that.

When the witch wasn't hissing and waving at Monkey to stop, she was watching the young man. With a twitch of an eyebrow and the tug of a corner of her mouth she endured his story. Part of him wished that she had not been there. But she always wanted to know more about his dreams, his adventures, and his past. Truthfully, after all these years, his experiences only felt real after he shared them with her.

When he finished, he reached out to her. She joined him and the two faced the dais, hand in hand. The young man looked to Tiger.

"You must get it back," Tiger said.

"Absolutely," Monkey said, tumbling to the ground. "Let's get all the hasty conclusions out of the way."

"It is clear."

"It smells, it's round, you roll it on the ground."

Poop, the young man explained to his lady with a sheepish grin.

—*I know.*

"You are not taking this serious." Tiger growled.

"No, I'm just not taking it how you like everything: burnt to a crisp and swallowed whole."

"What does it mean then?"

Monkey clapped his hands on his cheeks. "It has to mean something?" He slouched over in defeat. "How boring."

Tiger tucked his chin and shut his eyes. For all of Monkey's folly Tiger could usually hear what he was trying to say, eventually. With a rumble of breath he turned back to the young man. "Take your place up here, on the stones, young man, and tell us, what do you make of it? Was it flesh and bone? Or something from your fantasy?"

The young man shifted his feet, grappling with the inevitable question. "...It was real."

Tiger turned his glare on to Monkey, who frizzled beneath it.

"I think—at least, the important things," he added. The witch squeezed his hand.

"You must take it back," Tiger said. "Join us on the rock, young man. Speak to us, eye to eye."

"At least I can be glad there's *no one else* here," Monkey said abruptly, loudly, leaning in Python's direction. "—No one who might bring a different perspective to this conversation... some new, profound insight why not—?"

"If she wants to speak she will speak," Tiger snarled.

Python was already moving, a ripple of bright green cascading down her sleek form as she descended, coiling down her stone pedestal, an aloof nod in Monkey's direction. When she spoke her voice was deep, as smooth as velvet. Everyone listened. "It has always been a conversation among the animals, why the willows decided that man would be born without fur, fang, or claw. Even the plants can defend themselves in their own ways, with poison or concealment, with tough bark or piercing thorn. Why would the willows send out man naked and defenseless?" Her tongue flicked the air, her head swaying back and forth. "But there is a very old story which few care to remember anymore: the willows, loving man so, hid a Thorn deep inside of him so that he might bring it forth in times of great need. If this is true, then how can one steal a Thorn? And if this young man has lost his Thorn, who can reclaim it?"

"You must find these Lavanya and take back what is yours," Tiger said, his voice rising.

"And you must make more babies," Monkey said, mimicking Tiger's gruff voice. "Because, only two? Come now."

The young man stepped forward, shaking his head. "I can't just leave you all here. The raiders will be back. And if it's not them it'll be someone else." His jaw tightened as he cradled his wounded arm. "There's always someone else."

Tiger lunged to the edge of the dais and roared at the young man, shaking the very tress, his awesome rows of fangs exposed, his breath hot as fire. The young man pulled back, his fists raised, his heart pounding.

Tiger snapped his jaws shut. "Did you come seeking council like a man or permission like a child? Join us on the rock!"

"Not until I've earned it!" the young man said, tears running down his dirt-smudged cheeks.

Tiger turned his back.

The witch came along side him, placing her hand on his back. "We all protect our home, and our children."

Monkey bounded from the dais and tumbled to a stop before the young man. "Hey. Hey, sprout." He crouched low to catch the young man's eyes, now red and weary. "Watch my finger." He took his long, crooked index finger and drew it slowly toward his own face as he spoke. "If you want to go and search for this Thorn, we will guard the grove—we, who cannot leave, and your lady, who is infinitely capable. Or, if you never want to speak of it again, we will do just that." He slid his finger deep into his nose until it contorted his face. "But if you want to play 'Pull the Tail' with Tiger, you're going to have to wait your turn."

The young man let out an exhausted laugh.

Monkey drew out his finger and presented it to him. "Now, what does this smell like?"

"This is disgusting," the witch uttered.

The young man leaned forward, breathed deep, and said what Monkey had taught him, "It smells like majesty."

"You are correct."

"Ymrosch." Everyone turned at the sound of Python's voice. Her insight rose at random times, and often in no discernible order. "The Lavanya said that name. It is possible they were speaking of a child of Ymir, one of the primeval beings who gave birth to the Jötnar, the first giants. If this is so, Ymrosch is a very large, very dangerous creature, perhaps even the size of a mountain."

The young man nodded at Python. He smiled at Monkey. "Thank you. Thank you all. I'll think about what you said. Later. I will."

Tiger retreated into the night.

"Thank you, Tiger."

Tiger didn't respond.

"Get some rest," Monkey said with a wink. "You look awful." Then he flew up into the branches in a single leap.

Python had left as well. Or at least she could no longer be seen.

The young man sighed. He leaned into the witch, kissing her on her bare shoulder. She grabbed hold of his hand.

"Where's our boy?" he said. "I didn't see him this morning."

The young witch turned her head, eyes cast to the ground as though listening. She was reaching out to find their son, following the thread that bound her heart to his, just as it was with the young man and their daughter.

It only took a moment before she lifted her gaze. "You know where he is."

He ran his tongue across his teeth, behind shut lips. He nodded twice, and then left the circle of willows.

Ian Abdo

5

The young man dropped into the dim, root-lined chamber. The only sound was the air he sucked through his teeth. He held his wounded arm as he tried to stand. He hit the tangle of roots that hung from the ceiling and ducked again, a shower of dirt falling on him. He shook his head with a sigh.

> *Right,*
> *I'm bigger now.*

Besides the new, cramped feeling of the chamber, it looked exactly how it had been, years before, when he had chased a lemur down the long and narrow tunnel above. His throat constricted.

A faint crimson light touched everything with its marbled, shifting hues. It emanated from above the small figure who sat facing the far wall; a pearl of light, just like his mother and grandmother could make. His fair and nimble fingers reached up, scrawling a symbol on the flat, packed earth using a crooked stick. Long black hair and narrow shoulders, scrawny limbs that twitched with dexterity.

The young man had not known what to expect before his son was born. They thought that he might look just like his big sister. But there was something reasonable in the way their son, very small and fragile, came out looking just like his mother—except for his eyes. A brilliant green. But even they held a depth of determination the young man didn't see in himself.

"You know it's bad for your eyes."

The hand paused. The light grew, filling the chamber. The hand continued.

It took the young man a moment to readjust to the light, but soon he was searching the mosaic of symbols that covered the walls. Some were big and crude, others little more than a gouging in the soil. A few were refined, detailed. He had wondered what his son did down here.

Besides the sign-work there were now also tunnels that Python had burrowed through the root-lined chamber, an extension of her already vast network of underground passages found beneath the grove.

"Did your mother teach you all of these?" he said with a deep frown.

"Some of them." The hand moved to the next open space and started another. "Did sister ask about the sky again? She was being so bothersome while you were gone."

"Did you make her cry?" the young man asked.

"No."

"Be honest."

"I am."

"I'm going to check with her."

"Uh-huh."

Though his son remained facing the wall, working away at the new symbol, the young man knew that his hair hung over his face, limp and unkempt, his eyes narrowed in concentration, the tip of his tongue pressed between his short, flat teeth.

"It is not my fault if she did cry," the boy said. "Mother says if we leave the grove we will lose the willows' protection. We will grow old. It is not a difficult thing to understand."

"That's not the point, son. Look at me." The boy kept drawing. "Your mother and I have asked you to be kind to your sister."

The young man continued to glare at the crowd of symbols that surrounded him. He wondered how far he had ventured down Python's tunnels, carrying his disconcerting practice. His lady argued that he was a warlock, the first in millennia, and she would not deny him a proper education. The young man tried to be supportive. The boatman could have dissuaded her.

The boy was etching what began to look like a willow. "Tell me about the red tree again."

"Again," the young man sighed.

"You and Grandmother had just left Uncle Perdue," the boy began.

The young man plunged his fingers beneath the cool, damp soil, his mind sinking into the memories. It couldn't hurt to tell it one more time. Besides, his son wanted to talk for once. "... I was happy," he began. "— really proud of myself for helping Uncle. Grandma was kind enough to let me take credit."

The boy turned around, still sitting cross-legged, careful to keep his black skirt tucked beneath his legs and the tails of his red sash placed just so beside him.

"I had never seen so much destruction before," he continued. "It was awful... to learn that something like that could happen, anywhere, to anyone."

"Then you saw the red tree," the boy said leaning forward.

"But it wasn't really red."

"Right, it was giant and black."

"Huge," the young man said with the slip of a smile.

"What did the symbols on the tree look like?"

His smile faded. This was what his son was wanting to talk about: he had looked away when asking the question.

"I couldn't see them yet, remember?" the young man said. "Not until I touched it."

"After you touched it, what did they look like?"

"Son—"

"You told me before," the boy said.

The young man searched the chamber. The crowd of signs seemed to be staring back at him, watching and listening.

'Use every opportunity', the young witch always told him. Her words came to him as his frustration mounted.

He'll do better than me.

He took a heavy breath and began quietly. "Men had done those terrible things to the red tree. Men like you and me. They wanted the tree to be something that it wasn't. And when they didn't get what they wanted they stabbed the tree, carving their symbols into it. They hurt the tree, changing it into the terrible thing that Grandma and I found that day."

The boy nodded. "Mother said they were incompetent."

"I don't know about that. But their symbols changed the tree and burnt down the forest."

"Mother says that that is why I have to practice, to master them."

"... It's not that simple." The young man fumbled for the right words.

He looked down. He had been carelessly drawing his finger through the soil. It was the sign the red tree had given him. This was the first time he had ever drawn anything. Jerking his hand away, he stared in stifling horror.

The boy dug his stick in, deftly tracing over the sign. "Mother says that I am not like Man. She says that I am a rarity."

"She loves you very much," he whispered, dashing away the sign as soon as his son had finished. The host of symbols across the walls were watching him. He pressed down his fears, compressing them with a desperate strength, enduring the new weight that pressed on his weary heart. He would deal with them later, by himself.

The boy continued drawing, hunched over, his hair draped over his face. No matter how he grew and changed, or how quickly he mastered speech and gestures, the young man still saw the tiny, frail infant his son had been the day he was born. His fragile baby boy.

The young man watched him until he couldn't keep silent any longer. "I love you too."

His son shrugged. "I know."

"No, really. I love you."

"Yeah."

"I love you more than Monkey loves sweet root."

"Stop it."

"I love you more than Mother loves jewelry—more than Tiger loves talking."

"Father—"

"I... just can't stop myself!" he shouted as he pounced on his son. The boy squealed with laughter as he tickled his sides, shrieking and wriggling on the ground. It hurt in every way possible, but the young man was laughing too, a mad and booming cackle.

The crimson light flickered, pulsed brightly, and then was gone. The two froze in the sudden darkness.

"What just happened?" the young man whispered in mock-fear.

The boy giggled compulsively.

"Did I break something?"

"Get off of me," the boy whined.

The young man sat up with some effort, feeling every ache and pain seize his body.

The pearl of light reappeared as the boy sat up, shaking the dirt from his hair and brushing it off his arms and back. "You know I do not like that." But a laugh burst out of him as he tried to complain.

"Come on," the young man said. "It's late and I'm hungry."

6

The young man and his family gathered in the circle, beneath the great willow. Threads of deep copper and navy light cut through the clearing at a shallow angle. The fading colors of dusk settled all around them. The young witch and the girl had gathered a feast. Various berries, pomegranates, red curl-bark, and sweet root, all spread out on broad leaves.

"What do we say?"

"Thank you, mother. Thank you, sister."

They ate and talked. They laughed. Sometimes the young man dropped his food accidentally, his fingers refusing to finish the simple task. He tried to hide it.

"Ham hands," the young witch said dryly when she saw the dull ache of embarrassment on his face. He smiled back.

"Ham hands, ham hands," the children repeated without looking up from their meals. It was all the more endearing because they didn't know what "ham" was. He flexed his gnarled fingers. Too many years of training and combat. They were no longer fit to handle delicate things.

The girl soon made her way onto her father's lap. She fed him pomegranate seeds, one for him, two for her, and alternately played with his hair with her sticky hands. The boy remained seated upright beside his mother, asking questions. They spoke of Krejcarek and his raiders.

"Will they return?" the boy asked.

"We don't know, son."

"I would return, with a bigger army."

Neither the young man nor the witch felt like responding to that.

The girl told about her time with Tiger and her games with Monkey, standing up to act out the parts she found particularly hilarious.

"What do I always say?" she growled in her high voice as she strutted up one of the larger roots, her chest puffed out. The young man was already laughing, remembering how many times Tiger had lost his temper, scouring the ground with his claws and roaring at him with furious disappointment. His daughter crouched above them, chin held high, shouting, "Speak up! Speak up!" Even the boy smiled at that. The young man caught a glimpse of happiness shining in his lady's eye.

He tried not to look at his daughter's willow bracelet. He wondered how long the willows had held back, suffering this poor child to live without real protection.

Later, he told himself.
Don't do this now.

The boy reported on his studies and his time in the root-lined chamber. But it was difficult for the young man to concentrate. The voices of the young witch and her son drifted around him, articulate, contemplative, and insightful. His daughter had returned to his lap, playing with his hair and singing softly, disinterested. Maybe he simply wished his son to remain a child for as long as possible. A stupid argument, he knew. Especially since he was the one that had taught his son the sign of the red tree.

Not now.

Later.

The food disappeared. The last lights of dusk died. A swarm of silver pollen descended, illuminating the shadowed corners with its soft, clean luminescence.

They climbed the great willow, one by one. They passed the young man's first nest, the one he made when he was just a boy. Then they passed the nest he had made for the young witch for when she used to visit. Lastly, they came to their family nest, a mass of downy leaves and twigs cradled in a broad crook of intersecting branches.

With much sound and tradition, the girl found enough room to lie without being touched by anyone else, and the boy burrowed enough room between the young man and the witch, making certain a hand or foot was touching both of them.

"Tomorrow is a new day," the witch whispered, just as her mother used to say to her.

"Tomorrow is a new day," they all answered.

Bodies shifted and readjusted some more, rustling the thick bed of leaves and twigs. The young man removed his son's articulated toes from between his ribs a few times during the nightly ritual.

Eventually, all grew quiet.

The distant hush of streams.

The murmur of the night animals.

The groan of bending branches.

The children fell asleep. The young man was left in the dark, his arms wrapped around his fevered, aching body.

Not now.
You have to sleep.

But he had once again failed
to protect his beloved,
his children, and his home.

The Lavanya may have stolen more
than he had ever imagined.

The willows didn't trust him
to protect his own daughter.

He had lost Tiger's respect,
if he had ever had it.

And he had drawn the red tree's symbol,
for the first time in his life,
and he had done it in front of his son.

No wonder they gave up on me.

The young witch's hand caressed the side of his face. He shut his mind and shut his eyes, the burning of tears threatening to come.

Will you be able to sleep? her soft voice sounded in his mind.
Maybe.

His voice was hoarse as he whispered, "Are you happy here?"

"You are here. Our children are here. I am happy."

"Good."

He could feel her searching him, her silence like a question. He took hold of her hand, pressing it against the side of his face.

Not now.

But he couldn't stop the words: "Something's not right."

She was quiet.

"I can't go on like this."

"Do you need to seek your Thorn?" she finally said.

He cleared his throat.

"Speak the words," she said.

"Is that okay?"

"Speak the words, please."

He sighed. "I... want to see if it's out there... I need to know if I can fix this thing inside of me."

"You are injured."

"I'm ... I need to know."

Silence.

Then he heard the young witch nod her head, still lying on the nest. "I will be here when you get back."

She lifted her hand. He kissed it before letting her take it back. He had never felt so alone.

~

He reached for his lady. She was not there. His children were gone as well. Sitting upright, he squinted through the bold sunlight. The side of his face felt stiff. It was almost mid-day; he could tell by way the light broke through the canopy. They had let him sleep in. The dull pain of his body awoke as well, filling him, taking hold of every joint and muscle, making him question whether today was the best day to leave. The sounds of his family playing nearby tickled his ears. He sat hunched over for a time. His lady had left him to sleep because he needed it. But all he could think was,

It's like I'm already gone.

Unwilling to endure the nest any longer, he climbed down the willow to gathered his supplies: fresh and dried fruits, palm leaves, and roots for his satchel, and the black and green patterned cloak the young witch had made for him. He held it in his hands pensively. He had watched her make it. Dying the thread. Weaving the patterns. Her patience, her attentiveness, and tenacity. He tried to not marvel her openly. She gave it to him before he left on one of his early adventures.

"For when I am not beside you," she had said.

It took him a long time before he could answer, "Nothing is the same when you're not there."

He threw the cloak over his shoulders, pinning it in place. The grove seemed strangely quiet. He didn't see a single creature as he went about his tasks.

He went to the creek to fill the skin he had taken from a raider years before. He caught a glimpse of his reflection in the crystal waters. His crooked, hawk-like nose, his sharp cheekbones and sloped jaw. The general's venom had burned half his face, leaving it raw, coarse, and scabrous. It had melted the hair from the side of his head. He knew he wasn't beautiful like his lady, or her mother. He wasn't handsome like Perdue, or Tiger. Even so his heart sank as he examined his poor features. The hair would grow back. His skin would heal, for the most part. His body healed remarkably well, and quickly—at least that's what the young witch and his guardians always told him. But new scars would remain, a well-kept score of every one of his failures. He rose, unable to look at himself any longer. With all his gear slung across his chest and his cloak about his shoulders he wandered the grove searching for everyone.

He had left home many times through the years, but never like this. Never so selfishly. He didn't know what he would find. He might get to see the Lavanya. He might have to see the Lavanya. The first time he ever left home was to follow the lemur to the edge of the world. He kept falling into that loathsome day, over and over again, as though he was that boy again. He had left without saying good-bye to anyone:

> *He had been certain that saying goodbye*
> *would've been too sad to bear.*

Thoughts of a selfish child.

Never again.

He searched everywhere. The grove was empty. Mid-day passed. Downcast, he trudged towards the archway. But as he approached he heard them. And by the time he entered the clearing before the archway he knew what he would find.

Bear, deer, fox, and boar hemmed the clearing; squirrel, sloth, blue jay, and owl weighed down every branch. Hummingbird and firefly floated and flitted overhead. Tiger, Python, and Monkey took up one side of the archway, and his family stood on the other. The clearing erupted with celebration. Birds chirped, bears bayed, foxes cried, even the owls, who should've been fast asleep by now, added their voices to the acclaim. Monkey tackled the young man, gathering him up, lifting him onto his shoulders, and then paraded him before all.

The young man smiled broadly as he wiped the tears from his cheeks, but they continued to fall. Python seemed uncomfortable with the entire affair, but she endured it, her glistening, black eyes fixed on the young man. Tiger bowed low before him, and he bowed back, his hand pressed to his heart. Monkey circled the clearing twice before dropping the young man before the archway, and then wrapped him in a great hug. It was difficult to hear Monkey over the crowd, but he was fairly certain that he said, "I'm going to hide all your stuff while you're gone."

He had never held Monkey so tightly.

When they let go, he turned to his family. The young witch prompted their son to go to his father. Their daughter needed no encouragement. The young man fell to his knees as he took his children into his arms.

"I love you, I love you both," he said over and over again, the cheers drowning out his voice. He made himself say it, to keep from saying,

> *I'm sorry.*
> *I'm doing this for you.*
> *I don't know what I'm doing.*
> *I need to do this.*
> *I'm so sorry.*

He pulled back to look at his children. His daughter's worried face was covered in tears. His son would not look at him, his fair cheeks dappled pink. "Be good," he said, letting them go and standing, but the boy held on. He knelt once more, taking the boy in his arms, pressing their foreheads together. "Be brave," he told him. One last kiss on the head for both of them and he rose to face his lady.

He took her outstretched hand and they walked to the archway, shining with the afternoon light. The crowd had begun to lose its volume, and by the time the two had reached the curtains of branches he felt he should say something. Turning, he faced his family, scanning the brush and the high branches and all the faces that watched him, now growing quiet, now waiting expectantly. He fumbled for the right words.

"You all make me, better. And you make me want to be good ... That's what I'm going to do, try and make you proud of me."

"Our son will return a man!" Tiger roared. And the clearing erupted once more in celebration.

Tiger drew near. The young man had so much he wanted to tell him. Tiger spoke first:

"You have escaped nothing. You will join us on the rock upon your return."

"Yes, Tiger," he answered, containing all his hope and relief.

With a final wave good-bye, the young man and the witch walked through the shimmering archway.

The branches closed behind them, swallowing them in shifting shadows and ponderous, swinging branches. Very soon the din from the grove had faded to a harmless murmur, leaving little more than the sound of their breathing, and the hiss of the indifferent leaves against their bodies as they pushed forward. He wanted to speak to the willows, to tell them how he would make them proud too, how he would do better this time. But his good intentions felt world-weary, and his heart weary from such an unexpected farewell. One of Python's old sayings came to mind:

To know someone's lies, listen to them speak.
To know someone's truth, simply watch their steps.

He decided to keep his mouth shut.

The witch's hand was no longer in his. He couldn't remember who had let go. Reaching out, he found her. Fingers interlaced. But her voice didn't enter his mind. Tentatively, his face fixed straight ahead, he listened, feeling for her through the warmth of her skin. She felt so quiet, so still. He had to smother his own turbulence to make room for her subtle shades and motion. Only then did he begin to feel it. There was fear—he knew the flavor intimately—doubts, too. It was a muted, muddled mass of emotions walled up behind her indomitable will. Every fiber of his being urged to lean against that wall, to press his ear and to scratch at it. But the hard truth held him back: he couldn't bare to hear her naked thoughts of him at that moment.

The light grew hotter and brighter until they parted the final branches and walked out into the valley, the glaring afternoon sun beating down on them. His ears were ringing from the celebration they had just left. The pungent scent of battle and death still hung in the air. They stopped and faced each other. Her hair and makeup was elaborate that day, immaculate, as always, braided and tied up, something of a ponytail hanging off the side of her head. Her makeup was a contrasting combination of bold, broad, slashing stripes and painstaking, geometric ornamentation. She had painted a detailed design around her tear-shaped scar, a mixture of black and gold curls.

"You gathered them all," he said.

"I told the guardians. They did the rest."

He would have to let go soon.

"It was what you wanted."

"Am I doing the right thing?" he said, looking away.

A moment of consideration. "How about this instead," she said, resting her hand gently on his scar. "Do you think you are doing the best thing?"

He squinted into the horizon, his shoulders relaxing at her touch. "I think … I need to know, for certain …"

"Then so do I." She let go and reached into a small pouch on her utility belt, bringing out a toy pewter soldier.

"You should take him with you."

He smiled. "For the conversations?" He took the soldier and looked it over, like meeting an old friend.

"Because I cannot be there," she said. "In case you need help in finding your way."

He didn't know what to think about that.

"Why did he stop talking? You never told me."

"He stopped talking when he realized that you would do anything for me."

He pulled her close. "I'll be fast."

"You will be careful."

"Deal."

They kissed. He needed to remember how she tasted, the softness of her thin lips against his, and the earthen, pungent smell of her breath. He needed to take as much of her with him as he could. Then he held her again, her head on his shoulder. The day seemed to be slipping away.

Don't leave her.

"Okay," he said, but he didn't let go.

"Yes," she said.

Don't you dare.

He eventually released her, stepping away.

One last kiss, one last look, then he turned and marched out of the valley.

Ian Abdo

Part II

~

1

The young man traveled through forests. It was difficult to remember what to look for. He had made a point to never venture this way. But the days were warm and the nights pleasant. It was a quiet journey. Monkey wasn't there to interrupt with jokes and games, unfortunately.

> *Where did I ask the lemur*
> *about life and death?*
>
> *Where did I blindly believe*
> *every answer she gave me?*

He traveled through valleys. But nothing looked familiar. The days grew overcast. A stagnant chill fell over the evenings. The witch and their children weren't beside him when he laid down to sleep. He forgot to eat sometimes.

Where did the willow's bracelet
waste its power to protect me?

Where did I sulk and complain
like an ignorant child?

He traveled aimlessly through blustery grasslands. There was no reason to get up in the mornings. Tiger couldn't call him to training. He couldn't while away an afternoon listening to Python. No raiders were at his doorstep. There was nothing. There was no one. No one but himself.

Where were my guardians
when I needed them the most?

Where did I lose my way?

Not now, he told himself one more time.
                                                    Not now.

~

One evening he slowed to a stop beneath an old beech tree, unable to catch his breath.

"You followed her out here," he said, exasperated. "Why would you trust a stranger like that?"

All he wanted was to lay down. He pressed his forehead against the trunk. "Why would you trust anyone like that?"

He picked at the thin, pale bark. It flaked off and fell to the ground as if it had given up a long time ago.

"Not now!" His fingernails raked down the trunk, shredding it clean. He staggered away.

"Not now," he said, quieter, and more firmly. He stopped himself and shut his eyes. His hand had absently pulled the pewter soldier out from the fold in the waistband of his skirt. He held it tightly in his fist. He wanted to say it again, but the words had lost all meaning. Why had he started saying it to begin with?

My Thorn will change everything.

So he walked. Sometimes it was a tentative shuffle, sometimes a blind march. Sometimes it was tedious backtracking. It was all the same to him. Days were lost in searching, and nights surrendered to hollow, wasteful silence, the pewter soldier safe in his grip.

~

One day he stepped over a trickling creek. He stopped. He turned back. The creek had flowed from a short waterfall upstream, framed between a scattering of thin pines. It was a short waterfall. He could've crouched behind it. He walked upstream, looking at it for a long while. He sniffed the air. He bent forward, head cocked to the side. This was the waterfall he had walked under while talking to the old witch about life and death.

"Right," he whispered. "I'm bigger now."

He slowly turned, his eyes wide and searching. This forest was no longer a stranger to him. There was no comfort in that thought. But he set off with sure steps. Then it was a light jog. He swept the branches from his way with his good arm. He fixed his eye in the direction of the meadow—less than a day's journey ahead—and the Lavanya that he was unprepared to face.

A sound caught his ear. He crouched low. A rustling of leaves. The murmur of the nearby creek. A sobbing, a crippling, exasperated mewling. He snaked through the brush toward the trembling, high-pitched voice. The stench of death filled his nostrils. He freed his stiff arm from the sling and pulled back the final branch.

A great heap of bloody, dark fur sat in the middle of the clearing. Glistening patterns of red covered the floor of dead leaves. Next to the body sat a small creature, rocking back and forth, its face buried in its paws, smothering its frantic noises.

The young man crept into the clearing, checking every corner and shadow. The small creature was made of frayed, blood-smeared burlap, stitched together crudely with twine. It looked like a dirty sack, its contents pushing and bulging in strange places.

"Who else is here?" he whispered to the tortured thing. It slowed its rocking, quieting itself.

"Who did this?" he said, raising his voice.

He watched the creature in its recovery, still tensed, still keeping watch. The creature lay its paw on the wet, matted fur of the dead animal.

"Was he your family?" The young man could barely speak the words. His hand reached for his scar.

The creature lifted its burlap head, looking up at the young man with its mismatched button eyes; one of them hung loosely from shoddy thread-work.

> *My lady,*
> > *my daughter,*
> > > *and son...*

His heart shriveled. He stood upright, his eyes clouded with tears. But the meadow was close. He could feel it.

"You're not safe here," he said.

"Don't leave me." The creature lifted its paws to him, just like his daughter when she was ready to be carried.

He stepped back. "I'm sorry."

> *Take its hand.*
> *Walk away.*

The hollow silence compelled him. But he needed to hesitate, a furrowed brow and a moment of resistance, to prove to himself that he was the one making the choice.

He reached down, taking the small paws in his calloused hands and helped it to its feet. Its contents shifted, resettling with the movement.

"What should I call you?" he asked as the pain flared up in his bad arm.

"I answer to Sawdust."

The young man returned his arm to the sling beneath his cloak and held it. He looked to the dead animal. "I'm sorry for your family."

Sawdust touched the animal.

He could only offer a moment of quiet respect before saying once more, "It's not safe here."

Sawdust turned back to the young man and nodded. "I'm ready."

The two left the clearing, Sawdust toddling close behind him. The young man was walking away from the meadow. He was uncertain why.

The Lavanya are too dangerous, he told himself.

His eyes searched the shadowed, shifting forest. Sawdust was little more than the muffled clatter of its contents at his heels. Questions were following him as well: what attacked them? Where did they go? How did Sawdust survive? And why did this small thing seem to trust him?

"You shouldn't follow me much longer," he said.

"Why would you say that?"

"I'm going to find ... trouble."

"You don't strike me as foolhardy."

The young man couldn't answer that.

"What trouble awaits us?" Sawdust asked.

"Three creatures, called Lavanya."

Sawdust was humming to itself.

"They're evil creatures," he said. "—pretending to be nice when they're ... " He readjusted his bad arm. "They're liars. They're thieves. I hope you never have to see their horrible faces."

"You're looking for these things?" Sawdust said.

"They took something from me. I'm going to take it back."

"You sound thrilled to see them again."

"No. No, I'm not," the young man said firmly. His cheeks and neck felt hot. He was grateful Sawdust was walking behind him.

They didn't speak for the rest of the day. Only the colorful flash of an escaping bird, or a rare squirrel or snake disturbed their somber march.

~

They took shelter in the hollow of a chokecherry bush, the branches rising and curling around them like two cupped hands. As soon as they entered, Sawdust shuffled to one corner and plopped onto the fertile ground like a sack. The young man sat down with his back against the trunk, his elbows on his knees, fiddling with the pewter solider. The last lights of day pierced the branches, speckling everything within. The soldier caught these rays, twinkling with shades of rust and glaring orange. He couldn't remember the last time he had slept away from his family for so long. Each evening seemed easier than the last. There was nothing comforting about that.

"They said a name that I don't know anything about," he continued as though the conversation had never ended. "Ymrosch. I think. Someone I know says he—it —might be a giant ... tall as a mountain. I don't know."

"What's in your hands?" Sawdust asked.

He presented the pewter soldier. "A gift, from my lady." Then he closed his fingers around it.

"May I see it?"

His hand retreated, squeezing the soldier. "Should keep it close."

"Hm. Prudent."

Dusk faded, dimming the hollow.

"I've heard that name before," Sawdust said. The fading light made the clouds of dust gleam in the musty air. Sawdust seemed to be staring at the ground, its body sagging forward, its legs splayed.

The young man put the back of his fist against his mouth. It'd be too easy, wouldn't it? To have happened to find the one thing that could lead him to Ymrosch? He was missing something.

"We should try and sleep," he finally said. He tucked the soldier into the band of his skirt and wrapped the cloak around himself.

Sawdust didn't respond. Maybe it had already fallen asleep. He watched his companion for a long while before he laid his head back against the trunk of the bush.

Tomorrow's a new day.

But even as the words came to mind—bringing the faint smells of home, the distant voices of his family, and a fleeting warmth that made his skin feel even colder still—he didn't believe them. Something from today remained unsettled.

~

The young man woke with a jerk. He hadn't slept long. Shadows of the night filled the hollow. His arm had seized up. A dull ache burned in his bones, from wrist to shoulder. He gripped it with a groan, but then found it felt different. Something coarse and hard was hidden beneath the thin fabric of the sling. He pulled loose his arm. He had to raise it, awkwardly, drawing back his cloak, sniffing at it softly. The black, chitinous roots had expanded, crawling downward, weaving together to grip his upper arm. Smaller, scarlet roots reached down farther, webbing his elbow. A fresh musk scent, mixed with a faint sting of decay. He could hear a gentle, persistent creaking from somewhere within it. He thought he could feel it. He cradled his arm against his body, his mind churning.

He had been hurt so many times before: ax wounds, bullets, maulings, he had carried them all. But the Blackroot had never grown out before—not in a long, long time. He looked up, his head pressed against the trunk, watching the branches of the chokecherry bush.

What's different now?
What's happening to me?

His attention flicked to Sawdust, seated in its corner, just as it was the night before. He strained to hear beyond the branches and leaves that surrounded them. There was nothing to hear. No movement of ground or grass. No breathing. No smells—beyond Sawdust's musty scent, and the smell of his Blackroot, which had both intensified in the small space. It was as though the forest outside was empty. The chill of night braced him. He took in a deep breath, flexing his bad arm, and reminding himself of why he was there.

I've heard the name before.

Was it a trap? What was he missing? Either way, he needed to learn something about Ymrosch before he left. He could trick Sawdust into telling him. Shouldn't be too hard. He glanced to Sawdust's corner. It seemed to be asleep. Or he could just leave now. He hadn't wandered too far from the meadow. If he hurried he could make it there by evening. But the young witch would've stayed to help Sawdust—the old witch as well, to a point. Monkey would've stayed. He flexed his arm. Why did he want to leave? What was he missing? He readjusted fitfully.

"Time to go?" Sawdust asked.

He froze.

"Not yet."

~

Day broke. The young man stirred. So did Sawdust. He offered it some food.

Sawdust gave a polite wave. "I don't care for that sort of thing."

He put it back in his sling bag. "What do you eat?"

"Oh, this and that."

Under a mismatched-button gaze, the young man gathered what little he had. Then they set off. He was still walking away from the meadow. But as noon came and went he began to turn gradually, so he wouldn't have to backtrack as much. Sawdust stayed close behind, humming to itself.

"Where should I leave you?" he asked.

Sawdust continued humming.

"Do you know anyone who you'd be safe with?" he said.

"You, of course," it said.

He winced. "You know I'm going somewhere very dangerous."

"Don't you want to hear about Ymrosch?"

The feeling passed through him again. But he couldn't ignore the question.

"Yes," he sighed. "What have you heard?"

Sawdust hummed a short tune. "Would you mind if I had a look at that toy soldier of yours?"

He jerked to a stop, turning on Sawdust, "Why?" he raised his voice.

Sawdust stumbled to a stop. "Why not?"

He clutched his scar and glared down on the small creature that was taking him away from his home with nothing more than clever words.

Just like her.

He stepped back. He felt sick. "Why didn't you answer my questions, in the clearing, where I found you?"

Sawdust pushed on its contents, readjusting itself.

"Y-you didn't answer me," he stammered on, running his fingertips across his brow. "You just let me think ..." The air grew thin.

"Did anything attack you at all?"

"As I told you, my family shielded my life with his."

"What happened?"

"I smelled blood and bile. I heard all manner of screaming. Many different voices. It was terrifying—"

"—What was his name, your family?" he barked, stepping forward, looming over the creature.

Sawdust retreated, rubbing its paw on the side of its frayed and blood-flaked body. "Sunburn."

Just like before ...

"You're acting very suspicious," Sawdust said. "I only asked to see your toy."

"No, tell me about Ymrosch first, and then I'll let you," he said through set teeth. His fist was trembling.

Sawdust flopped onto its bottom. "Oh, I would've gladly, yesterday. But I don't know if I can trust you now. You understand."

"Just stop it," he gasped, pulling at the collar of his cloak, taking a couple steps back. "Just—I know what you're doing. I'm not a child anymore ... I'm not ..."

Sawdust watched him, its head tilted to the side. "What's wrong with you?"

He twisted, fumbling, running from Sawdust, stumbling violently through the forest, crashing through brush and branches, his heartbeat throbbing in his ears. He couldn't tell if he heard laughter behind him. Maybe it was just the sound of his own harsh and manic breath.

Ian Abdo

2

It took the young man several days to make his way to the meadow. He shuffled despondently from the treeline into the tall, brown grassland, all the while glancing over his shoulder. He wasn't certain he had found the right place. A distant and spiteful sun glared down on him. The rocky ground swelled into bald hillocks here and there. The gray, gnarled oaks that ringed the clearing were all slouched, beaten down by time and temperature.

"Where are they?" The words died on his cracked lips. He turned about, searching the desolation. He breathed in the muggy air. It swept through his cloak, sending it billowing out. At the far end of the meadow, hidden among the shadows of the oaks, two glowing red eyes watched him. He looked over his shoulder once more and then back at those unblinking eyes. They were low to the ground. His hands closed to fists at his sides. His blood pounded in his temples.

"Come on!" he said, throwing his cloak and sling bags to the ground. His arm ached. "What are you going to try? I'm not afraid of you!"

The eyes swung side to side, as though whatever they were attached to was readjusting its footing.

He stared back for a few more moments, then stomping away.

The pond had receded to little more than a brown puddle, surrounded by smooth stones and cracked and pitted soil, packed flat from when it used to lay beneath the water.

The hollow hung in an unnatural darkness. There didn't seem to be anything of interest in there, nothing moving, nor anything strange to draw his attention. The young man remained outside, in the seething sunlight, stepping side to side.

He wandered the surrounding forest where he had played with the young girls, and laid on the grass with them, their limbs entwined—where he had listened to them and let them care for him—where he had adored them. There was nothing left. Altogether abandoned. His chest ached.

He reached the treeline of the meadow. An electric-blue coyote stood over his heap of bags and cloak, sniffing at them. He shouted. She looked up at him with those bright red eyes. She almost looked like she was grinning.

"That's mine! Get away!" He sprinted at the coyote.

The coyote bolted at him, a deft blur of color.

He screamed at her with every breath he took, pushing himself even faster.

Never again.

He pumped his arms. His Blackroot was on fire, a swarm of needles snaking through his bones. She slipped between his hands. She locked his skirt in her jaws. The fabric tore. His waist was wrenched backward. He lost his footing. The side of his face struck the ground.

He gripped the dry soil, his head swimming, and pushed himself to his knees, only to fall back to the ground.

The coyote huffed. He squinted up. The gleam of polished pewter shone from between her jaws. She darted away, disappearing into the oaks.

He rolled over onto his back and fumbled to re-pin his skirt, his fingers refusing to cooperate, his sight fogging with tears.

I'm a failure.

He secured his skirt as best he could. He shuffled to his things, grabbed his cloak, and hurried as best he could after the thief.

~

They traveled through fields, valleys and hills, deserts and dense forest.

> He ran.
> He stumbled and fell.
> He got up.
> He walked.
> He cried.
> He gave up.
> He tried again.
> And not always in that order.

The coyote never got far. She was a fleck of blue on the horizon, forever looking over her shoulder at him. Somewhere in the back of his mind he wondered why that was. But he wasn't in his mind. Day and night his body followed hers. The sun was blinding, the moon refused to shine, and neither was tolerable. He wasn't sure what he would do if he caught her. His own thoughts seemed to rise up against him every time he found an ounce of momentum.

Why did you let me leave?
You knew I wasn't ready.
Do you even like me?
Would you miss me if I never came back?

His legs numbed. His heart burned. His breath slowed, ragged and shallow. His feet struck the ground, one after the other, jarring his skull.

~

One evening he found himself jogging through a wide and rolling field of yellow dandelions. He suddenly felt the emptiness of his body, and the frantic urge to push on despite himself. The coyote seemed to be outpacing him today. She seemed to be sailing through the flowers with particular speed, the thousands of delicate petals flaking free, taking flight in flocks, swirling into waves in her wake. As he had not done for a very long time, the young man looked up. A mountain rose before him, framed by an ominous, cloud-choked sky of black, white, and gray. It was a grim thing that blotted out the horizon, covered in snow and pale blue ice, with a few rashes of black and bent trees scattered across its face. The peak disappeared into the slow-swirling clouds which haloed it.

Soon he could see the coyote was heading for a campsite nestled at the foot of the mountain. A faint flicker of a fire caught his eye.

As they approached he began to see tents, boxes, patches of color hidden beneath the cover of trees. Sweet aromas found him on the wind. Wood smoke, savory spices, and vanilla.

The coyote reached the camp. She sat down facing him, her back to the campfire. A dirty young gypsy watched him from beyond the fire, arms and legs crossed as she leaned against one of the boxes near the tents. He made himself slow to a walk, to approach with caution. There was something familiar about her. She wore a top hat with a peacock plume sat cocked to one side on her head. Long and wavy blond hair tumbled down her back to her waist. A black lace choker was around her neck. She wore a black dinner jacket over a faded scarlet blouse, and a long, many-layered skirt of autumn colored patches.

He came to stand before the coyote. The pewter soldier rested on the ground between them. Exhaustion wrapped him up as soon as he stopped, an impossible weight. The coyote looked back at the young gypsy, panting, a grin on her face. Then she trotted away.

He slowly bent to pick up the soldier as he watched her bobbing tail retreat.

"I despise the very sight of her," said the gypsy.

"Who is she?" he gasped, struggling to catch his breath.

"She is a fly in the ear."

"... I didn't know."

"Well now you do."

He took in the whole campsite, still trying to place her. "Where am I?"

She held it as long as she could. Then guffawed, throwing her head forward as she clapped her hands. "You don't recognize me, do you?"

He stepped back, his legs trembling.

"You've filled out, I'll tip the hat, but you haven't changed a stitch have you?"

"Who are you?" he said, trying to make his voice sound stronger.

One more scrutinizing gaze, top to toe. She pushed off the box. "Welcome, young man, to the foot of Ymrosch."

He looked again to where the coyote had disappeared, baffled.

How did she know?
Why would she care?

"Girls?" the young woman called. "All clear."

Two more gypsies stepped into the camp:

One of them, topped with pigtails, had jammed her fists into the pockets of her patchwork leather vest. A short, double-layered skirt of scarlet swung around her wide hips as she swaggered by. She was sucking a toothpick, rolling it side to side with her round teeth.

The other one, tall and timid, hung back near one of the tents. She wore trousers, suspenders, and a deep-cut, sleeveless tunic. A silk scarf hung loosely around her neck. She had a limp mohawk, her wild locks falling over the side of her head, hiding one of her wide, doe-like eyes.

"How did he find us?" said the tall one near the tent.

"Coincidence took him for a romp, didn't she?" said the one with pigtails through a round and toothy grin. "Next time I'll have a rock on hand. Cop her square on the snout."

"Are you going to tell him?"

"He's not ready. Look at him."

He cradled his wounded arm beneath his cloak.

The top hat gypsy raised her arms like a conductor. "Ladies, gentleman. Sit, please. Let's discuss the matter."

No one moved.

He couldn't believe it. But the more he stared at them, the less he could deny it: They had piercings now, tarnished silver and wood earrings, nose rings, and the timid one had gauged ears. Their clothing was torn and faded. Even their skin, though obviously clear and smooth beneath, was matted in makeup and smudged with dirt and soot—but still, he recognized them. The words came out before he realized it:

"You're the Lavanya?"

"Calling us Lavanya is like calling you Man," the timid one called out. "How would you like that?"

He frowned at her.

"Call me Ro," said the first gypsy, touching the brim of her top hat.

"Sham," said the one with pigtails, lifting her chin at him.

"I'm Beau," said the one by the tent, waving.

"We've been expecting you," said Ro.

All at once he remembered their soft skin, their claws, the sound of their laughter, their scaled flesh and terrible speed, and he stepped back again. He had been so certain that he was ready to see them again. But they had grown up into young women. He turned his head, hiding the burns on the side of his face.

Ro stepped toward him hastily, "We know what you have come for, but, regretfully, it is no longer in our care." Sweeping to one side, she pointed up at the mountain and said, "He has it."

"The pronoun game?" said Sham. "Such a tease." She gestured slowly to the mountain: "This mountain is Ymrosch."

"—He's slightly smaller than the mountain, truly," Beau explained in her soft tones. "A host of stone and stuff has covered him, just so you know. They say he gave up one day, just sat down and the mountain grew on top of him."

He lifted his eyes, traveling up the treacherous slopes, the black and craggy rock formations, and the burden of clouds that haloed the higher, snow draped region. It was the highest mountain he had ever seen. He closed his tired eyes.

"Oh, he'll never make it," said Beau.

"Sham, will you fetch it for me?" said Ro.

Sham shuffled to one of the tents, threw back the flap, and slipped inside.

"Ymrosch is very old," Ro began, catching his attention as she stepped up to the fire, opposite him. "— Thousands of pages old. Son of Ymir. The Bitter One. Maker of Vales. Feast of Orjus. The Flesh Army of Crescent Bay. He won't give back your Secret, not willingly."

Sham closed the tent flap behind her and approaching the fire pit with a bundle of leather in her arms.

Ro continued: "I—we—have a gift for you. A tool to help reclaim what once was lost." Ro accepted the bundle from her sister with great care.

What you stole.

"I don't want it," he said.

"Told you," Sham sang.

Ro clucked her tongue at her sister. Then she circled the fire, standing before him, every motion artful and steady. "Aren't you the least bit curious?"

The firelight splashed across her face. Her pixie smile. Her eager and searching eyes. The years had only complemented her. He remembered why he had never wanted to leave the meadow. He looked away.

"Are you so confident you can face him alone?"

A sneer flicked across his face. He huffed. He flexed his bad arm. He turned back to her.

The leather felt thick and supple between his fingers. Cream and bronze, with a few blood-colored swaths. She helped him open the folds, one after the other, until he found the gift inside.

It was a curved short sword, brutally weathered and scarred with countless chips and cuts. A swirling pattern of scales covered the handle, with lengths of tentacles wrapped taut in a woven pattern across portions of it. A large amethyst was set where the handle met the blade, fixed there by tentacles and clasp-like fangs. The blade itself was dull black steel, laced with bruise-colored veins.

Sweat beaded his forehead. His vision blurred. The sword seemed to be giving off neither heat nor cold but something else entirely, and it robbed both feelings from his face. He glanced up at Ro. There was something about her face, something he had never seen in her before. It was a fugitive shadow. Then brazen intensity returned to her eyes. "You'll never have to fear anyone ever again," she said.

He took hold of the handle.

The ground opened beneath his feet, dropping him into endless wind and darkness. He let out a sound but his voice was sucked from his lungs. Twisting in the free-fall, he reached out, swiping blindly for anything solid. Wet and frantic things wriggled up his throat. His body convulsed. He tried to scream but his throat was pressed full of twisting, coiling limbs. They sprang from his mouth, wrapping back around his face, his neck, pulling at his skin and his hair. The ground raced toward him. He couldn't see it. But knew it would meet him. His body tensed more, and more, his heart wailing under the anticipation. His head was nearly covered, wrapped in this living, grasping mask, squeezing his skull. He stopped trying to breathe. But it hurt worse than the effort to try. The ground was coming. But it wasn't ground. It was water. A black, fathomless lake. And something was waiting for him beneath the surface, something immense, an eternal, maddening hunger. He let go of the handle. He staggered backwards, collapsing to the ground, shivering and retching. The Lavanya's voices swam around him:

"What happened?"

"He doesn't look too good."

"You said he wouldn't know."

"He shouldn't have... Oh."

"He's Esmane, isn't he? Brilliant.

"How did *you* not know—"

"—Shut it."

"You took this," he finally said, trying to catch his breath, spitting the acrid taste from his mouth. "You took this from someone else, just like you took something from me."

The gypsies didn't answer him.

He rose shakily to his feet, stepping back. "Get that thing away from me."

Ro folded the leather up again as she stepped back.

He thought he saw something moving at the edge of camp, among the bushes. He squinted.

This intruder, she almost looked like the Lavanya, from before—young, small, with short, strawberry blond hair, and dressed in sheer scarlet—though she was dirty, and her face was strained by concern.

"How many of you are there?" he demanded, wiping the hot sweat from his brow. "What do you want from me?"

Ro snapped her head about. "Onus, leave."

"Is he okay?" Onus asked, tugging at her dress.

"I won't say it again."

"Who is she?" he said pointing and raising his voice.

Ro turned back to him, her cheeks ablaze.

"She's our sister," Beau said.

"Just tell him," Sham said.

"He won't care!" Ro shrieked, hurling the bundle of leather to the ground in a fit. "I told you so many times, nobody cares. He's here to get what's his. He's looking out for himself. We're just a problem to him. A mistake —and yes, maybe I deserve that, but I do everything for you. I have done everything for you. I don't care if the whole book hates me I would do it all over again. Leviathan take my Secret, I would die for all of you."

The sisters leaned away from Ro, every mouth shut, every eye cast to the ground. The young man despised how full his heart felt for her.

"We know," Sham muttered, folding her arms. "We do."

"Ymrosch stole Onus from us," Beau told the young man with an urgent kind of sorrow. Ro started toward her sister but then retreated just as quickly, wiping a hand across her mouth. Beau, throwing furtive glances at her sister, continued, "—He swallowed her whole, you see, a keepsake in his belly. He said that he would only give her back if we brought him the power to set himself free."

"My ..." He didn't know what to call it.

"Your Secret. Precisely," Sham said.

A question struggled to form in his mind. Ro answered before he could find his voice:

"You were the first thing we came across potent enough to please him."

The words were a hot brand against his chest.

"It was like that in the beginning," Sham added. "But the time we had with you—"

"No," he heard himself say. Too much of him wanted their words to keep washing over him. "Just, stop."

Ro strode sharply to her box and slumped back against it with arms crossed. "Take the sword, leave the sword, your Secret is up there—" she nodded at the mountain, "—with him."

The young man twisted a thumb and finger around his wrist as he looked to the mountain.

He had finally met the Lavanya again. He couldn't remember why he had wanted to so desperately. He wanted to look at them. He didn't want them to see him looking.

There seemed to be a path to the right of the camp. He touched the pewter soldier, once again tucked securely beneath his skirt band. A shiver of guilt. There was nothing left to say. He turned to leave.

Onus stood before him. In her hands she held a pair of boots and gloves, all fine, dark leather, fur-lined, as well as a blood-red scarf. Now, suddenly so close, he could see she looked exactly like the Lavanya from all those years ago. She didn't look much older than his son. His heart withered.

She started to speak.

He tried to walk around her.

She stepped in his way.

He moved to shove her away but recoiled instead, raising his fists over his head in aggravation.

"For the cold," she said, timid and yet persistent, offering the clothing to him.

"It will be cold," Sham assured him.

"No," he said vehemently.

Onus's chin sank.

A hesitation, a momentary struggle, and then he put out his hands. He unclenched his fists, receiving the gifts from her. She was looking up at him with an earnest gaze. He marched off.

"Make him suffer," Ro said

"Make him suffer," Sham said.

"Make him suffer." Beau's voice was quiet, but he heard it distinctly, even beyond the light of the camp. Dusk had come, carving out the darkening sky with brilliant shelves of crimson and navy. Soon he was alone, with nothing but the stillness of evening to accuse him.

He checked over his shoulder now and then. He couldn't imagine why they might follow him, but he looked just the same.

Ian Abdo

3

The path was smooth and wide in the beginning. Soft soil and big, flat rocks. He thought that he passed over the Lavanya's camp at one point, the faint aroma of campfire and spices seeming to rise up from somewhere far below. Pine trees sometimes bordered the way, but it was the paleness of the soil that helped him to keep the path, especially after nightfall. His feet ached. Soon his knees started complaining. The scarf draped easily around his neck, but the boots and gloves were awkward to carry. He considered dropping them more than once. He wished they would've invited him to rest at the camp. But no one should trust the Lavanya. He wished they had offered him food. He hoped he wouldn't have said "no".

The longer he walked the more he came to understand the size of the mountain. Though he covered much ground, climbing the switchback trails, negotiating the various terrains of jagged rock, broad streams, and sweeping grassland, it remained looming with abominable indifference, its ice and snow patches glowing in the dark of night.

The moment the first dirty lumps of ice began peppering the trail he sat down and put on the boots and gloves. He hated snow. The boots were surprisingly comfortable. He felt guilty because of how well they held his poor feet. But even with the boots he moved slowly, rationing what little strength he had, uncertain of what he would find at the top, if he ever made it there.

The wind whipped about him. The air chilled, making his breath into white vapors. The dandelion fields seemed far below now, a good sign of progress. The patches of ice became bigger, thicker, covering whole sections of the trail. A soft, feathering snowfall dappled his cheeks with their cold touch. Dizzy with exhaustion, uncertain of how far he had left to go, uncertain how long until dawn, he had no choice but to find shelter.

A small cave of black rock appeared on the horizon. He stumbled the last few paces, but he managed to crawl inside. Seated crookedly among the rocks, the pewter soldier in his fist, his head against a cold piece of stone, he let out a pitiable sigh.

He wondered what his lady was doing just then. He held the soldier against his chest. Did she know that he had been excited to see the Lavanya again? Did she doubt his love for her? It didn't matter what she thought. He knew the truth. All the times he had let her down. All the ways he was less than what she deserved. The list of shortcomings trailed all the way back into their childhood. All he wanted to do was make it up to her. He had been trying to make things right for years now. But even the smallest victories were eclipsed by the constant parade of mistakes, like the parade of scars that covered his body. He closed his eyes.

~

Long ago, when he was just a boy and she a girl, they played without end. Exploring, talking, and climbing. Running about, chasing after each other, hiding and jumping out to scare one another. The grove had never been so loud with joy. One day the girl found a particularly clever hiding spot. Once the boy had passed she leaped out, startling him. He spun about and accidentally struck her on the side of the face with his elbow.

There was blood. She cried. He screamed for help. Monkey came and took care of her. The boy told her how sorry he was; he said it many times that day. That wound became a tear-like scar on the outside of her eye. She said she forgave him. But he still felt horrible. The days passed. He kept apologizing. She continued to forgive him. He brought her beautiful rocks and fallen leaves, told her Monkey's funniest jokes, and entertained her with Python's most charming riddles. She seemed happy. He couldn't let the feeling go.

One day, with his fists against his stomach, he came to her and apologized one more time. She didn't answer. She wouldn't face him. He said it again. She walked away. He followed her for a while. Finally, she ran out of the grove.

Heartbroken, he went to Monkey, but Monkey shooed him away.

Next he went to Python. Python listened attentively, patiently, until he had folded to the ground in sobs. She waited until he had poured out all his tears and then said,

"To know someone's lies, listen to them speak. To know someone's truth, simply watch their steps."

"I don't understand," he said.

She considered for a long moment before saying, "Did she accept your apology?"

"Yes."

"And do you plan to hurt her again?"

"No, never. I'll never hurt her ever again."

It almost looked like she smiled. "Then there is nothing else to be done."

"But why do I still feel so awful?"

"I'm sorry, but I cannot help you."

He ran away and hid.

Tiger had to come and find him. He was particularly afraid of Tiger at that time.

"Little sprout!" Tiger called up to him in his most famous secret hiding place. He had to call a few more times, eventually threatening him in order to roust the boy.

When the boy had climbed down to the ground and explained what had happened, Tiger said, "She has already returned. I saw her down by the creek."

"She did? She is?"

"Did you think that she was gone forever?"

"I don't know. I thought maybe … I didn't know."

"Apologizing to others takes courage, this is true. But there's another step, something that will take all the determination in your heart, something you failed to do."

"What is it?" he begged. "How do I fix this?"

"You forgive yourself."

He began to cry again. "But," he sobbed, "But what if she only said she forgives me and then I mess up again and she tells me she really didn't forgive me? What if she leaves for good?"

Tiger laughed loud and long, startling the boy. "And what if she lingers forever? You should be more worried about that!" he said, still reining in his laughter.

When he had finished, and recomposed himself, he looked sternly at the downcast boy. "How do we meet the enemy?"

"Be simple. Be direct," the boy recited, still lost in turmoil.

Tiger gave a curt nod. "And how do we travel in times of war?"

"Travel light?"

Another nod. "Take only what you need."

The boy was trying to puzzle together what Tiger had just told him, all while snuffling and holding his stomach.

"I'm telling you to let it go," Tiger said. "It's no longer useful. But—and listen closely —if you don't find the courage to forgive yourself, you will drive her away for good. You can rely on that."

He opened his eyes. A silly story. His tired mind must have been wandering. He readjusted with a grunt, trying to find the position where the least amount of rocks stabbed at him.

He woke at first light, his temples throbbing and his back stiff. The cold air coated his raw throat as he took in his first breath. His right arm felt heavier. He took hold of it beneath his cloak, massaging his Blackroot. The chitinous roots had grown, covering his entire upper arm and cradling his elbow. The smaller, scarlet roots now twisted about his forearm.

There was something alive inside of it, something just below its chilled and rutted grain. A silent, dreadful promise. He couldn't remember how long it had been there, how long it had slept inside of him, waiting until this moment to wake up. Had the Red Tree given it to him? Or had it always been there? Worse than that, he had no idea what would happen if it got out … if he set it free.

> *It's changing you,*
>> the Boatman had told him.
> *I don't care about that,*
>> he had replied like a stupid child.

"Stop changing me," he whispered to the Blackroot.

Hollowed out by hunger, frustrated by his shivering limbs, he couldn't lay still for another moment. He dragged himself from the cave. The mountainside seemed serene that morning. The cloud cover made it feel like evening. Slopes of pure ice and snow shone with an unnatural glow all around him. The wind had died during the night, leaving the sparse trees limp and motionless. Fields, rivers, hills and forests, the grand scene spread out far below him. Home lay somewhere beyond his sight. He didn't want to start walking. He turned and set one boot in front of the other, his head hung low, watching only the trail before him. The uneven crunch of his boot-steps felt so loud.

Soon he entered a forest of dark pines. The shadows stole what little warmth he still had. Ice gradually coated the way. Banks of hard snow reared up on either side. Black rocks were scattered among the trees. The air felt close, and he could hear every little noise he made, his frail steps, his rustling skirt and cloak, and his shaky breath. The path remained well-defined, a knife-stroke through the tall and sickly pines. A lane of blinding white hung over his head. He wondered who had made the lonely trail. It was well-trodden, and wide enough for one large creature.

> *The Lavanya visited Ymrosch often,*
> the thought crossed his mind.

But why would they? Unless this was a trap. Maybe they had his Secret the whole time, and have now sent him to a pointless death. But why would they do that? What would they gain? It's not that he thought they were trustworthy. He didn't know them at all, he knew that now. He wanted to think of them as the three identical girls he had met all those years ago. Simple. Awful. But they had never been simple. Sawdust wasn't simple. Neither was Coincidence. Maybe they had finally told him the whole truth. He found even less comfort in that.

Ice hammered the right side of his head, throwing him to the ground. Something warm splattered across his face and mouth. He rolled about, grabbing at the heavy thing, pulling at it, trying to shake his head free, to find the strength to stand. The sounds of many scissors snapped in his ear. The thing writhed and clawed at him in a frenzy, clambering for new grips of flesh or hair, and slicing both in the process. Threads of pain raced over numbing skin. The sounds of his gloves shredding in the effort. His face burned from cold. With an agonizing shriek he ripped the thing from his head with both hands. Through blood-stained vision he stared up at a spindly fractal of ice trapped in his grip.

He pushed himself upright. He lifted his arm to throw the fractal away. It flexed, closing back around his hand like a vice. He crumbled beneath the shock. He scrambled to his feet, kicking up ice and snow. He lunged at a tree and drove the fractal into it. The echoes of ice striking cold wood fluttered through the forest. He struck it over and over again. The fractal tightened its grip. With a desperate cry and a final blow he broke the tree in two. The fractal sloughed limply from his fist. The top half of the tree crashed to the ground. He had barely staggered backward and the crippled fractal was skittering toward him again.

He ran. It was already right behind him. He tore loose his cloak. The fractal snapped into the air, flying at him. He turned, casting his cloak over it as he dropped to the ground. The cloak shot overhead, crunching and clattering as it hit the icy trail, tumbling to a stop. It twisted and hopped about frenetically inside, slashing away at the durable fabric.

He tumbled off into the snow bank, into the pines, and found the largest stone he thought he could carry. He planted his feet. His right hand throbbed in agony. He heaved the rock from the deep snow.

His cloak was nearly ribbons when he returned to it, the stone in his hands, gasping for breath. The stronger threads of the fabric had kept the spastic fractal ensnared. Raising the stone high above his head, he drove it into the ice fractal with all this strength.

He dropped to his knees, falling against the stone, panting, bleeding. He lifted it and smashed the shattered fractal one more time. He slumped to the ground.

His breath slowed.

Ymrosch's army travels this way.

His body shook uncontrollably. He had to move. Standing carefully with the help of the stone, he looked down at the shredded tangles of his cloak.

I've lost her.

The soldier was still tucked inside the waist of his skirt. He checked. His left hand and glove were only slightly cut and bloodied. His right glove had fallen off somewhere. The hand was covered in bright blood and deep, pink slices. He wrapped the scarf around it, tying it tight enough that he could feel his heartbeat in it.

One last look at the cloak, and then he moved on.

I lost her a long time ago.

His pace was even slower now, his boots dragging along the ice. His right arm hung limp at his side. He strained to lift his feet over the smallest root or mound of ice. He looked back, watching the stone in the middle of the path grow smaller and smaller. He was drizzling a trail of blood behind him.

> *The Lavanya won.*
> *They were always better than me.*

The trees dissipated before him until he was bathed in the full haze of the day. The wind rose like a temper.

Why did she tolerate me for so many years?

He groaned every time he stumbled.

Snow fell as he climbed another field of jagged rocks.

I'm slow.

I'm weak.

After that came a sloping field of flattened, dead grass. He fell. The bitter wind chafed at his bare skin. His right hand twitched with every beat of his slowing heart. Blades of grass poked at the cuts in his face.

Tiger would be disappointed. Python would never understand. Monkey would never tell him the truth. They expected so much from him. Especially her. She would leave, if she hadn't already. And even if she hadn't left she wouldn't be the same once he returned. It's the way it was always going to be.

A couple of tries, then he rolled over onto his back.

I'm going to die here.

He pulled the pewter soldier from his skirt and tucked it into his left glove, resting it in the palm of his hand.

Move, you child.

He dragged himself to his feet. His legs moved forward. His lungs drew in the cold air. His unfocused eyes were pointed at the path.

Give up or move,
you failure.

He held fast to the soldier, his fist pressed against his thigh.

~

The young man stood on a ridge of the mountain at the end of the trail. It ran into a highway, a wide and well-salted dirt road, stamped into the mountainside by legions of boots. The clouds had dissipated, leaving a blinding, blistering sky. It caused him to squint and raise his good hand to cover his face. The wind pushed his hair, tossing him about. The curious sensation of bone-chilling cold mixed with the grievous heat of the morning sun. The highway swept down the mountain, back and forth, disappearing behind a few hills and then reappearing again a ways off. Eventually, thin as a hair, it was gone. But he saw where it was leading:

Far below lay a crescent bay, surrounded by a sheer and colossal curved wall of blue ice. A city was tucked into the heart of that bay. He could tell from such a distance that it was massive. Thousands of soot-black buildings with dirty-yellow thatch roofs, crooked and pointed towers. Countless fortresses like fists rose above the houses. Rope bridges covered every possible gap.

Pressed against the wall of ice, there loomed a castle. Cruel, complex, and imposing, it seemed to be the source of the infection of Crescent Bay. Its many towers and buttresses pierced and wove in and out of the ice, fixing the tall and convoluted structure secure beyond removal.

It took his eyes a moment to readjust, but then he saw that the city was alive, the streets packed with creatures moving to and fro. Some of them seemed enormous compared to the commoners. The rope bridges were equally bustling. He saw fleets of long ships with full sails of every faded color, sign, and sigil. They came and went from the innumerable slender piers that reached out from the city's edge out into the black and shimmering waters. The smallest, faintest of sounds tickled at his ears. The creaking turn of waterwheels. The hush of running waters. The smeared, tireless moan of so many distant voices speaking all at once. Snaps and cracks and howls, the signs of labor and craft-work. The bay no doubt magnified and sharpened all of this, allowing him to hear any of it at all.

The mountain highway, however, seemed clear of travelers—and certainly of any armies.

He looked unsteadily to the mountaintop. The highway wound upward, searching out the easiest paths, and eventually plunged into a cave near the very peak. His destination. He stepped down onto the highway, a momentary sense of relief. It was almost over. The salt crunched beneath his boots as he began his final march.

Blinding white haloed his vision. He wrapped his arms around his bare and shivering body. Ice fractals of every size were scattered across the highway. Some of them were shattered, others simply lay there, twitching. Cold air battered him about. The cave. That was all that was left. His eyes ached as tears fought to come. His bones grew frail. His heart shriveled beneath the sun. His skin withered and flaked from his body.

Then he was standing before the cave, seeing it and not seeing it. That yawning entrance, like a great shark's mouth, and the long and winding tunnel that plunged into the mountain.

Small and weak.
Cold.
Afraid.
And lost.
So terribly lost.

Give up or move.

His fingers closed around the soldier.

He stepped into the cave.

The air turned even colder. The circular tunnel was cracked, ribbed, and strewn with chunks of ice of every size. Stalagmites and stalactites thrusting from floor and ceiling. It twisted right and left, sometimes rising and falling. A thin fog rolled along the ground. The glare of the sun faded the farther he shuffled into the tunnel until it finally died, leaving only the pale blue luminescence that came from somewhere inside the ice. It alone lit the way, bathing everything in its delicate, sterile glow. A low rumbling shook the ground. Two labored pulses followed by a silence, and then it began again. The sensation was so deep, he was uncertain when it had begun. His body had stopped breathing. He tried to take in the biting air. A short shudder and a grunt was all he could manage.

A breeze caressed his face, the scent of copper. He thought he heard a sound and he stopped his shuffling. All was quiet. He swayed uncontrollably as he strained to listen, his body trembling. Then it came again, frail, metallic words carried on the wind: "My flesh … Oh, my flesh …" Then it was quiet.

He continued.

The rumbling swelled. He felt the pulsing through his boots. It quickened.

Every step forward was a mistake. He looked behind. Any step back would be a mistake as well.

The breeze grew. It became a strong, putrid wind rushing past him and then barreling back down the tunnel. He bent his knees, but he couldn't help but falter before the rising gale.

"My flesh! My flesh!" the iron voice cried, a fleet and frozen keening that struck like a blow; he toppled to his knees. The tormented voice wailed on. He had to take hold of the stalagmites and the walls to make progress. The violent wind spiraled the fog; it cast about sheets of frost and a hail of ice shards. After much strain, he came upon a bend in the tunnel. Squinting through the torrent, he could see a shining, pale blue light from somewhere beyond the turn, casting its brilliance across the rippled walls. He prepared for another feeble effort forward. The wind stopped. Ice shards fell, skipping over the icy floor. Fog hung like vapor in the air. The rumbling had become a feverish pounding in the walls.

The voice came again, crashing through the tunnel, battering the walls, tearing down sheets of ice, roaring,

"Have you come for my flesh?"

4

Slowly, cautiously, he stepped around the bend, his hand on the wall to support himself. Before him was a massive and desolate banquet hall filled with broken pillars, long and icy tables topped with ruined decorations and scattered plates and silverware. The extravagant feast, now black and shriveled on their plates and platters, made it seem as though no one had taken a single bite—if anyone had attended the feast at all. The grand and arched vault was high as an oak, and the hall was twice that length. There seemed to be no exit. The far wall had crumbled. Iridescent blues and whites radiated from that broken, slouching mass of ice. Curtains of ice lay at the foot of the wall, sheets and fallen pillars piled up against it, covering its lower-half. A short, misshapen block protruded from its very center. And deep cracks covered everything above the slopes, radiating from that block like shattered glass. The top portion of the wall jutted forward, an overbearing shelf that ran the whole length, casting the area beneath in shadow.

He removed the pewter soldier from inside his glove. He took one more look around the hall, frowned at the soldier, then returned him to his waistband.

The young man searched the empty hall, wandering between the long tables. Something was there. It felt like home, though no home he had ever felt before. But their was something else too, something even heavier, older, stale and sick with unrest.

The lights dimmed, grew, and shifted, causing the whole room to look like it was moving. His nostrils and mouth felt coated in copper. The rumbling grew louder. He kept moving. The sounds of his shifting skirt. The crunching of ice beneath his boots echoed off the high ceiling.

He searched for a way through the broken wall, setting a foot on the icy hill. In the ruins he saw what must have been a wide doorway, before the collapse. Two small, deep tunnels had been punched into the wall on either side of the crooked block of protruding ice, just below the shelf. He stared at them for a long time. They contracted.

The doorway opened, lifting itself. A deafening voice cried out, "What do you want from me?"

The young man endured the blast of cold and rancid air. All he could utter was a gasp.

As big as a mountain.

The wall contracted, the cracks deepening. "Who sent you? Pinhook? Or was it trundle?"

The young man almost said "the Lavanya". But even then he knew that would've been a mistake.

"A coyote," he said, "—named Coincidence."

"—I do not believe you, Old-Child," Ymrosch bellowed.

Rattled, the young man could only think to ask why he called him that name. The giant persisted:

"Have you come for my flesh?" The hall grew even colder, and the stench of bitterness hung thick in the air, gathering about the young man.

The question seemed simple enough, which made him second-guess it. "… No."

"The Goatmen come for my flesh. They cut at me. They take my flesh to fight in their petty disputes." He sucked in a torrent of air. "You want something. You are all alike. What do you want?"

"The Goatmen? From the bay?" the young man said, beleaguered, working for every breath.

"Everyone takes from me. What do you want? Tell me what you want!"

The young man cringed, turning his head from the deafening fury. His legs threatened to give out.

"My Thorn!" he said. "Do you have my Thorn?"

Cold silence. Ymrosch glared down at him, his glistening, spiteful features hard and lifeless.

A sensation washed over the young man's brittle skin. It was the feeling of home again, only different—a fragile spark of warmth, reaching out for somewhere nearby. He tried to resist it.

It's down below,
inside him,
where he kept Onus.

He didn't think it.

The understanding came from somewhere else.

The lights dimmed, and the black pits of Ymrosch's eyes widened. The rumbling—his heart beat—lurched erratically and with great labor. The long and bitter cracks of his face flexed, wincing. With the screech of ice grinding against ice, he muttered a single word.

"Lavanya."

The young man tried to speak. Ymrosch let loose a deafening roar of fathomless contempt. It shook the young man's skull. He fell to the ground. Blinding white and blue lights. The hall rocked. The floor buckled, jutting up and sinking here and there, throwing him about. Massive sheets and pillars of ice crashed to the floor. White powder fell, casting eddies of blue and white haze all across the hall.

Everything settled. The young man didn't know where he landed. But he was forced to lay there, unable to find the strength to stand. His ears were stuffed with a deafening whine that made him squint. He couldn't feel the ice he lay upon. But Ymrosch's heartbeat rippled through the broken floor, racing through his numbed body.

It's impossible.

The scissor-sounds of skittering ice.

Ymrosch's voice reverberated all around him, pummeling his ears, as though it came from his own head.

"You will take my flesh, Old-Child. And you will be grateful for it."

The young man tried to rise. The haze was too thick to see anything. A clatter of volatile steps and then something overshadowed him. A lance of ice fell on him. He moved. Pain ripped through his pauldron. He rolled away. He scrambled to his feet, running haltingly, blindly. Behind him, the squeal of ice being pulled from ice.

"Tell me how grateful you are." The haze swirled about, dissipating from his tempestuous breath.

A pillar appeared to his right, leaning against a crumbled wall. He raced for it, scrambling and lunging over the chaotic ground.

Make him talk more.
Make him clear the air.

"I'm going to take it from you!" he screamed, not believing himself. "I've come for what's mine!"

Volatile footsteps clattered right behind him. He slid beneath the leaning pillar. The lance plunged through it, barely missing his leg. A spindly creature of interlacing ice shards towered over him, bobbing erratically, twitching. It was made of three lance-like legs, with a fourth one arching overhead from its back, now thrust through the pillar.

It twisted the lance. The pillar shattered. He scurried away, launching himself back into the haze. The hiss of a blade. A flash of pain leaped across his back. He hit the ground, rolled through, and staggered awkwardly to his feet.

"Do you hear me?" he moaned. "I'm going to take my Thorn and you can't stop me!"

"You do not know what pain is. But I promise, I will teach you all I have learned."

The haze flew away, dissipating, sweeping clear most of the hall. He stood near the exit. He turned. The ice creature crouched at the opposite end, before the giant's face. It shivered once, and then burst forth, rolling and skittering at him.

I can't do it.

He lifted his right arm, wincing as he clenching his mangled fist, the blood squelching from the drenched scarf, dribbling down its tails, sliding down his forearm, speckling the ground. Nothing happened. He looked to the wide slash in his Blackroot pauldron. Thick, dark sap oozed from the wound. Maybe he had lost that too. Or maybe he was afraid to let it out.

"Come on," his voice trembled. He took hold of his injured hand, forcing his opposite thumb deep into the tender wounds, gouging out every inch of pain he could find, to break free that dreadful promise. "Make him suffer."

Make him suffer.
Make sure he will never forget you were here.
Do something, for once in your life.
You're going to die here.
And everyone will be better off for it.
Make him suffer.

He let out a desperate scream. White hot torment exploded in his chest, tearing down his arm. Blood like fire raced through his legs with sickly strength. So much fear. So much more rage. His vision narrowed, his whole body roiling with hysteria.

The ice creature's lance flew at him. He struck it down with his fist, driving it into the ground. But it wasn't his fist anymore. The tangle of charred Blackroot had extended up his neck, around his upper back. And it had reached all the way down his arm, weaving together a clawed gauntlet that now armored his wounded hand.

The ice creature jerked and writhed about, frantic to free itself. He hammered the lance deeper into the ground. He marched between its flailing legs. Tearing off one of those legs, he beat it against the ground. Then he spun about, shattering it to pieces against a fallen pillar.

"My flesh! My flesh! My flesh" Ymrosch screamed.

The young man charged at that hard and bitter face. The ice creature was already snipping at his heels. To the left of Ymrosch another creature was fumbling to its feet, a swarm of ice fractals still crawling about it, awkwardly binding themselves into its gathering wholeness. He clamored up the sheets and pillars of the icy beard. Ymrosch collapsed his mouth to rubble, his broken features cut deeply by understanding and enmity. The young man pivoted, launching himself at Ymrosch's shocked eye. He had slid half-way in before it fell on him, shutting out the light.

Ymrosch's wails boomed through the ice, deafening him. He wriggled, clawing with his gauntlet, inching through the passage that worked to crush him, forcing the air from his lungs, pinning his other arm against his body, his shoulders shoved against his neck. Something battered his boots. Pain licked at his calves. He kicked at it. It came after him again.

No, his body said with every gain.
No, his lungs said, fighting for every sip of stale air.

He managed to wriggle the rest of his body into the eye. It must have been the ice fractals on his heels, following him inside. He felt their spastic flaying through the leather soles. Each pull forward cost everything. He couldn't hear what Ymrosch was saying —his hearing had grown achingly dull, his head, heavy —but he understood perfectly. The giant's rage and horror railed through his body, ravaging him to the bone. He kept his muscles taut to fight against the cold pressure on every side. His hips cramped. He hit the side of his face against the ice. He screamed because he couldn't do anything else. The fresh blood felt hot on his temple.

The tunnel expanded, throwing rays of light past him. He dragged himself forward furiously, one arm thrown over the other, panting through the effort, his eyes closed and his teeth clenched. The ice fractals swarmed, skittering up his boots and then his legs, digging their knife-like limbs into flesh. He found a drop-off at the end of the tunnel, pulled himself to it, and hung his head over the edge. Far below, at the bottom of a very long and warped well, feeble green lights illuminated a cavernous space. Ymrosch's belly.

Home.

Yes, his arms said as they pulled him over the edge.
Yes, his body said as it let go.

The rancid air flew past him. It howled in his ears. It threw about his knotted hair. He struck the sides of the shaft. It jarred his limp body with every impact, sending him twisting off in different directions, dashing to pieces the ice fractals that still clung to him. His eyes stung from the wind. He remembered falling in his vision, at the foot of the mountain. It didn't seem as real this time.

His arms reached out, flailing, clawing. With every blind impact his fingers grasped for edges or cracks to grip. He tore away curled ice-shavings and clouds of powder to descend with him. The air moved too fast to take in a full breath. Green lights grew brighter. They swung across his blurred and fluttering eyes.

The claws of his gauntlet swung like an ax to pierce the wall. They were spurned. His body reeled. The green lights approached. His body struck another ledge. He spun off again.

Then it happened. His rotation was right. The distance was perfect. His waist twisted. His claws extended. He struck the wall. The shriek of claws slicing through the craggy ice. Powder and shavings spraying over him. His other hand gripped the gauntlet for support. His claws extended even deeper. His momentum slowed. The well opened. He dropped into free-fall. The ground rushed at him. Swirling, green lights. He braced himself.

Ian Abdo

5

Ice rained down. He could hear it smashing against the ground all around him. Moving his head, he could feel that he lay on his back. He opened his eyes. A glittering cascade of ice fractals tumbled down form the well above him. They twirled, striking the walls as they fell, dropping to a harsh end on the uneven cavern floor where he lay. One struck his leg; he felt it in the bone. He clawed to his feet, stumbling away, his arms over his head. He fell against the cavern wall with a crunching noise.

A faint green haze lit the cavern with rippling, shifting hues. Only a few corners and edges remained drenched in darkness. The fractals dazzled like stars as they continued to fall, shattering, collecting in a pile beneath the narrow entrance high above.

A concentration of light pulsed from the far side of the cavern. He rose and made his way around the edge of the chamber, toward the light, tracing the wall with his claws as he limped along. The ice fractals had already begun to stir, a fitful undulation across the growing, gleaming, spindly mound. He approached the light and pressed his hands against the wall. It lay deep within the ice: an insignificant glimmer far beyond reach. It flickered. It flinched, dulling beneath his gaze. He stepped back.

What if I can't free it?

The skittering of dozens of ice fractals tickled his cottony ears. He grit his teeth. He drove his gauntlet into the wall. Fractals battered his body against the ice. He grasping at them, twisting about. He flung them away one at a time. He beat his back on the wall. They squealed beneath the impact.

The pile at the center of the cavern continued to grow. They flew at him in dazzling waves, pelting his ragged flesh. The rapid, hollow knocking of the fractals against the Blackroot. He shattered them in the gauntlet's grip. He tore them off his skin and skirt and beat them to shards against the wall. A crack appeared. He fended off the ravenous swarm, and focused what little strength he had left to widen the weak spot. A fresh wave wracked his body. His face struck the wall. He slumped to the ground, his vision dimming to red haze, his hands over his head. And still they poured onto him. Batting about his limbs. Scissor-snapping in his ears. The warm sting of a hundred cuts.

What if it doesn't want me?

Through the endless shimmering waves he glimpsed the remaining fractals clambering over each other, wrestling, binding together into a growing, lurching shape. He fought to his feet. He turned back to the crack in the wall. Blow after blow, he broke it wider. But his bloodied arms slowed. His sight was blurred.

What if I don't really want it?

They scratched and scraped at his Blackroot. His gauntlet broke through the ice. His knees gave out. The ice creature rose over his crumpled body. Its many, shivering limbs surrounded him.

"It's mine!" he wailed. "It belongs to me!"

The limbs stopped.

The ice fractals stopped.

His words echoed through the cavern, his mind altogether addled, his breath drifting from his lips like white silk.

Every ice fractal wriggled free from his body, falling to the ground with a clattering sound. He hissed at the awful sensation. They skittered away, giving him a circle of space.

Another trick?

His body was trembling. His taut skin felt like it was on fire. He lay slumped against the wall for a long time, his Blackroot pauldron turned out, his legs tucked against his body, waiting for them to do something. Anything.

They all stood watching him, each one leaning forward intently. The distant rumble and creaking of ice echoed darkly all around him. The fickle shifting of green lights and shadows. Only the erratic pulse of Ymrosch's heartbeat marked the passing of time, a rumbling that made the whole cavern shudder. He rose, using the gash in the wall to pull himself to his feet.

Has to be a trick.

He stared down the bed of fractals with a sneer. Even the broken ones, from the awkward chunks to the smallest splinters of ice, stood among the ranks.

Something tugged at his arm. He found a tooth of ice was still jammed deep into the back side of the gauntlet, stuck. He pulled it loose. It was lovely the way the light caught its many facets. He crouched with a groan, setting it on the ground. The tooth rolled back and forth, gaining momentum, before it tumbled away into the bed of ice fractals, where it found its place and shot upright, looking to the young man. He understood. He turned to the wall, to the dim light beyond.

They want me to take it away.

He raised his Blackroot gauntlet to strike at the ice once more. But then he saw it. White ice crystals clung to the crevasses, between the glistening, horned plates. Crescent-scores marked the dark and cruelly-patterned carapace. Sparkling pearls of sap traced the few delicate lines where it had been fractured. The two long tails of the crimson scarf hung from the wrist, torn, soaked in blood, and marbled with frost. He stared bleary-eyed at that ruthless thing.

He tugged the leather glove from his other hand, tossing it away. He opened his bare hand. It was calloused, lined with many cuts and scars. The knuckles and the tips of his fingers had been gnarled from years of abuse. But it was his hand. He offered it to the fading green light beyond, placing his gauntlet behind his back.

"Here I am," he whispered, and felt even weaker for saying it.

The light guttered.

He wanted to pull his hand back. He resisted.

This is how she would do it.

"I will take care of you," he murmured, keeping still.
The light died.
He shivered in the dark, choking back a sob.

I knew it would end this way.

The bed of fractals would swarm soon. He strained his aching ears to hear any movement from behind, preparing to turn and fight, to be shredded beneath their onslaught. But they made no sound. His wandering eyes adjusted to the darkness. The light hadn't died, not entirely. Its meager glow could be seen, a ghostly smear struggling against the utter blackness.

It's broken.

Of course it's broken.

He leaned forward, his hand reaching. "Come with me," he whispered. "You are mine."
A deep crack and a squeal. The handle of a blade burst through the ice. He took hold of it, pulling a dagger free from the wall with an arc of blazing green light.
The light flooded his body. He breathed in deeper than he had in years. It was almost too much to take in. The light was sound, cool, supple and strong, flowing through him, out of him, lacing every bone, muscle, and sinew, filling something he never known had been vacant, or maybe he had just become too comfortable with the emptiness. He wanted to throw it from his sight.

Don't trust it.

It won't last.

But this was only fear. He gripped the dagger with all his strength. His Thorn. The light took root inside; it grew, illuminating the cave, reflecting off the walls and shimmering in the air. The light was heavy. He had never felt so true. My Thorn. He couldn't contain it.

He burst into laughter, howling and staggering about. He screamed in delight, holding onto himself until his cheeks were wet with tears. His jaw and his sides ached with delicious pangs.

Finally, with a deep sigh, he stood upright, coughing, chuckling, wiping his eyes with the back of his bare hand. He found his reflection in the wall. His eyes shone like fire, his skin aglow. He looked over his shoulder. The bed of fractals had retreated, widening the circle around him, ever attentive, each one reflecting his verdant lights, adding their myriad colors to the glowing cavern.

He reset the band of his skirt and cleared his throat. "Thank you," he said. For some reason he was surprised that his voice was his own—full and commanding as it echoed off the ice, but still his.

He looked up. The well loomed high above, the only way out. He spun the dagger around in his hand as he turned to face the wall. He lifted his Thorn overhead and plunged it deep into the ice. Setting his boot into the hole he had made earlier, he lifted himself up, driving his claws in, higher up. Dagger, then gauntlet, and then dagger again, he worked his way up the wall. The long rhythm of the work carried him; readjusting his grip, holding his body close to the wall, searching the ice for the next solid patch to pierce; the lunge and the dull strike of the blade, or the cut of the claws as they pierced the wall. Sometimes his boots could find no purchase, so he hoisted himself up by his arms alone. The wall sloped inward, narrowing toward the neck of the well. His pace slowed. But his Thorn held, and the claws pierced deeply, even when his legs could only dangle beneath him. He knew he could make it. He didn't think about it. He simply gave himself over to the work.

When he had reached the neck of the well he took hold of the lowest ledge, dragged himself up onto it. He slumped to the ground, leaning against the wall, his eyes closed and his head back, letting his burning arms lay limp and restless at his sides. The ice was comforting to his lower back, now hot and slick with sweat. He kept wiping the sweat from his brow with his bare forearm. It dripped down his nose and the sides of his face, irritating the cuts all over his body. The bruise on his face was tender. His stomach turned with hunger. His hand absently squeezed his Thorn's handle, grimy from dirt and sweat. It sat in his grip as though it had always belonged there.

His eyes fell, finding his Thorn. It was a leaf-bladed weapon, elegant, pristine beneath the thin layer of filth that filled its cracks and crevasses. The handle was made of smooth ironwood, with slender ivy wrapped taut in a woven pattern around it. A shining, blood-red ruby was set where the handle met the blade, fixed there by circles of vines and a clasp of three thorns. The blade itself seemed to be made of polished steel, inlaid with the vein-like pattern of a leaf.

She would love it.

You don't deserve it.

"Get up," he told himself. He craned his neck sideways, to stare up the long, warped well. His light couldn't reach the top. His Thorn could make the climb, but his arms shook when he lifted them. And he couldn't forget, Ymrosch waited for him at the top. His eyes fluttered and closed. Sleep weighed heavy on his brow. A shiver swept over his cooling skin. His pauldron constricted.

You won't make it.

A sharp breath. "Get up!" he growled, and struck his armored elbow against the wall. His body felt heavier for the outburst.

He forced himself to stand. Shallow strips of skin tore loose from his lower back and the back of his bare shoulder, frozen to the wall by his now freezing sweat. He felt the relief of the pull, not the pain of it. He stretched his arms and shook out his feet. The boots hung like stones tied to his ankles.

He looked to his Thorn. "You'll have to carry me ... at least part-way." His stomach dropped, but the dagger still felt as though it belonged in his hand. So he turned, facing the wall, and began the impossible climb.

~

Sometimes he found the rhythm. Sometimes every reach was like lifting tree trunks. A couple of times he had to hang there, unable to find any kind of reserve. The ledges along the way were small mercies at the beginning. Toward the end he avoided them, seeing nothing but the temptation to sit down. Occasionally he had to use them, to shake out his hands, to catch his breath, to give himself time to recover. But he always pressed on as quickly as possible.

One time the claws didn't hold. He dropped a long ways, landing hard on a ledge far below, bruising his knee and ribs. He had no choice but to lay there until his eyes could focus and his lungs could pull in a full breath. Quiet sobs echoed off the walls, a high pattering that danced down the long, dark shaft. He wept longer than he wanted to. In this place there was no grove. There were no willows or guardians, no family or raiders. He was alone with a single problem, and a lifetime of mistakes. He could handle that.

~

He was kneeling at the back of Ymrosch's mouth, his shoulders slumped forward, his fists on his thighs, swaying and trembling. No more light came from his body. He could remember climbing, but it had become a single memory—a moment of simple work, and simple patience. He didn't feel particularly connected to any of it, nor could he remember the cost. A dusting of golden sand lay strewn about him. His eyes dropped closed. He sucked in a desperate breath, forcing them back open. He growled, planted a boot on the ground, and then pushed himself to his feet.

The mouth was a wide tunnel with an arched, ribbed ceiling. Blue lights shone through the far wall— Ymrosch's lips, collapsed shut. The ceiling dropped, crushing the wall down even farther. It sounded like a spiteful sneer. He staggered forward, almost falling twice, and set the spiked knuckles of his gauntlet against that uneven wall.

"Let me go," he said, his voice thin and quavering. "Why won't you just let me go?" He laid his forehead on the ice. His reflection stared back; pallid skin ravaged by wide cuts and angry bruises, a slack jaw and a bloodshot eye. He looked away. The ice moaned deeply, steeped in anguish. The dull crack of distant, shifting ice plates sounded all around him. Somewhere inside he was only waiting to prove what he already knew. Time dragged on. His heart cooled.

He jabbed the ice with his Blackroot fist, stumbling backward. "Always one more thing to do!" he wailed, stomping about in his frailty, shaking his gauntlet. "One more problem! Always!" He laughed and screamed and swung his arms like a marionette. The room spun. A tearing pain in his lip. Fresh blood found his tongue. His Thorn grew heavy in his hand. It wasn't a dagger anymore. It had transformed, with sounds of cracking branches, reaching and lengthening, until it had become a war hammer. It was an ornate weapon with a long staff. The ruby was set into its sleek and deadly head. He took it in both hands, strode to the wall, and used all his momentum to drive the hammer into the ice.

The cave rocked. A wind raged about him. He crouched to steady himself. The potent taste of copper filled his nose and mouth. He could even feel the flavor on his skin. His Thorn had bitten deeply. He had to work it free. Then he drove it into the wall again.

The wall crushed down on itself even further, the ice glowing brightly with its sterile blue luminescence. An iron voice shook the cave, devastating, indiscernible, and reeking of pain.

Make him suffer.

He was smiling as he swung the hammer again. And again. And again. Deep cracks blitzed across the hardening ice, radiating out with every blow. Ymrosch wailed furiously. So he struck even harder.

Tiger would be proud.

The words chimed somewhere deep inside him. But that was a lie. His footing slipped mid-swing, the hammer glanced off the ice. He staggered back, letting the head drop to the ground at the end of its swing. Golden sand shifted and scattered beneath his unsteady footsteps. He took a moment to catch his breath.

How sad.

He swept a bare forearm across his forehead, but there was no sweat. His bruises stung. The skin was flaky to the touch. Every muscle trembled. Laughter tried to leap from his throat. A frail cough was all that came out.

How very, very sad.

The ceiling dropped once more. He turned away as the wall was pulverized. Ice and powder blasted out at him, dancing across the ground. The white haze settled. He stood upright to find broad striations of the wall had been crystallized. The hall lay bare before him, beyond the layered shelves of shimmering, translucent windows: the fallen pillars, slumping walls, and the havoc the flesh soldier had left, and, at the far end, the tunnel leading back to the surface of the mountain. His escape. Somehow he knew—his Blackroot knew, his Thorn knew—Ymrosch had made the ice wall too hard. Hard enough to shatter.

He heaved the hammer from the ground, dropping it back into both hands. He spun about, bringing every ounce of strength he had to his final, vindictive blow. His Thorn pierced the glass. The wall buckled with a sharp rupture, blowing out in the most satisfying way, blasting shards all across the hall.

Wind tumbled past him as he crawled through the ugly hole he had made. He slipped and scrambled unsteadily down the lose ice beard. He then turned and started walking backwards toward the exit, the hammer firm in his grip, a scowl fixed on Ymrosch. But Ymrosch wasn't looking at him.

The giant seemed even older now, dim, and filthy. His face had sloughed down. His eyes were crushed shut. A twitching, struggling map of torture. The hole in

Ymrosch's mouth was more ruinous than he had imagined. Cruel, blackened cracks reached out over his features. The largest of them cut diagonally, up through one of his eyes.

"Just like all the rest," he slurred, powder and icy debris slobbering from his grotesque wound. "Take it, you insignificant speck, you petty thief—"

"Your permission means *nothing*!" the young man retaliated, shaking the war hammer at him.

"It has always been this way, Old-Child. Are you pleased to believe that you are the first to ever take something from me?"

Make him suffer.

The young man decided that silence would be the perfect response. He continued glaring as he made his way backward toward the tunnel. A trail of rolling, golden sand and speckles of dark blood was left in his boot-prints.

Ymrosch tried to speak, his face twisting in effort, seizing with spasms of impotent rage. None of the ice fractals emerged from his face. No more flesh soldiers appeared. Still, the young man twitched at the slightest sign of movement.

He finally reached the tunnel. Ymrosch wouldn't attack. He could see that now. He turned to leave.

"Wait." Ymrosch's voice had changed. It was smaller, soft, and halting.

The young man stopped, setting the knuckles of his gauntlet against the side of the tunnel to steady himself. He waited, his back to the broken giant, to make him him speak again—to plead, one last time.

"How did ..." the giant slurred, and then hesitated, "Why ... Why wouldn't it work for me?"

The young man turned. "Because you think it's a *thing* to be used," he spit out. He didn't hide his exhilaration. But his words were a lie. "Think about that for the rest of your life, you failure."

He trudged out through the tunnel, away from Ymrosch and everything he had done there.

Ian Abdo

Part III

~

1

Dusk met him when he reached the mouth of the cave. Or maybe it was dawn. His breath billowed from his lips like steam. An aching-warmth wrapped up his body. Clean, cool wind washed over him. The sky lay as clear as when he had entered, though he was uncertain how long ago that was. Ebony water expanded into the haze of the horizon, a smooth, slightly curved plane reflecting the rice-paper sky.

"I did it," he whispered.

Or did he let you go?

His cottony ears perked up, catching a sound that must have been there the whole time. The wind made them elusive. He squinted and tilted his head. The crunch of many, many pairs of boots pounding over the salted highway. The rhythmic clapping of different kinds of armor—leather and steel, perhaps. His muddled mind identified it all at once. Several horns rose into his line of sight. He threw his haggard body from the highway, toppling into the snow, buckling through the tough crust to the pillowy fluff beneath. He lay silent, mostly buried in the burning-cold. Soon the army began marching by, their boot-laces in arm's reach.

The Goatmen.

He could see why Ymrosch called them that. They were ranks of thick, filthy, and pungent warriors. They wore elk-horned helmets of every shape and size, and snarling, ghoulish masks. Braided beards of raven hair burst from beneath these masks. Proud mantels of straw and fur laid over their hauberks and jackets of gleaming scales and aramid. He saw spears, axes, assault rifles, and handguns. A few warriors carried flamethrowers, their fuel-packs strapped to their backs. Their blue pilot lights were ignited and hissing. He knew that sound well.

An ashen-haired child marched among them, unarmed. He could not have been much older than the young man's daughter. This child held his narrow gaze fixed forward and his wide, square chin lifted high. His skin was bruised, scared, and weather-beaten. His make-shift uniform was made of skin-tight leather with patches of some sort of shimmering scales and stripes of aramid, a well-adorned utility belt, and one streamlined leather pauldron, trimmed in fur. A leather thong about his neck held many silver rings. They danced on his chest; their padded chiming took the place of his silent footfalls. The young one was surrounded by a cadre of thick-necked Goatmen who kept the pace, holding tight formation around him, their assault rifles ready across their chests.

The ashen-haired boy marched by the young man laying in the snow bank. The child turned his head and found the young man's eye. The young man gripped his Thorn. The boy winked at him and continued on.

The rest of the army worked its way into Ymrosch's mountain. The sounds of their grunts and their boot steps echoed from inside the tunnel.

He was alone again.

The young man rose stiffly to his knees. The ashen-haired boy seemed to have recognized him. But the young man couldn't place him.

Why did that disturb him? Why should he care? He didn't care. What had he missed? What had he forgotten?

He climbed up the cumbersome bank and shuffled down the highway until he returned to the small trail he had used on his way up.

~

He trundled down the sloping field of flattened, dead grass. The gray wash of clouds covered the sky once more. He couldn't remember when it had happened. He kept looking over his shoulder. Ymrosch could be anywhere. How far could his flesh soldiers travel from the cave? Had they attacked the Lavanya's camp? He quickened at the thought, fumbling hurriedly down the uneven field. Something wasn't right.

No, they had to still be there. They were too clever to be killed by the flesh soldiers. They were smarter than that. If anyone deserved to punish them it had to be him. He wanted to be the one to make them feel pain—that awful, gnawing pain of regret. Because they ruined him. But that wasn't the truth. But he would find them there. He just had to make it down the mountain.

Next was the field of jagged rocks. He tripped constantly. The hillocks of many-sized stones shifted beneath his boots, sending him falling again and again. Every time he struggled back to his feet, disoriented, bruised and bleeding, the hammer held before him. He strangled its staff, alert as he could muster. He turned about, watching his back, brandishing his Thorn. Golden sand spilled from its head. What was he afraid of? He had taken back his Thorn. He was going to the Lavanya's camp next. No one could stop him. Let them try.

That's a lie, isn't it?
You're lying to yourself.

Managing the rocky terrain, setting hand over hand, setting one boot after the other, he had little to do but think. Something wasn't right. He stolen his Thorn from Ymrosch. Someone could steal it from him. The icy wind cut at him. He turned his face from it as he pushed forward. Someone could steal it from him again. Everything he ever lost was taken from him. He got what he has because he took it from someone else.

Anything is right,
if you're powerful enough.

An exasperated breath.
"You sound like the old witch."

The forest of dark pines rose around him. He didn't notice until the long shadows clung to his skin. It was as though he had never left. He stared down the stark and endless corridor. The high banks of hardened snow on either side. The black stones scattered among the black and spindly trees. The blazing white cloud-cast sky overhead, and the barren silence, making every noise harsh before snatching it away. He marched on. He knew he would walk by the his shredded cloak. He knew he wouldn't even glace at it. And once he had left the dark forest he didn't want to think about why.

He thought about seeing the Lavanya again. He was ready. That was a lie. There was also the curved sword. He could take it now. The Blackroot was sure. His Thorn was silent. He would be so strong. Even the old witch would have to respect him. Maybe she would even be impressed. Was it too much for him? Of course not ... But why would he want it anyway? He had his Thorn. He had earned it. Had he earned it? What would he do then, return the sword to its owner? Why should anyone get his Secret back so easily? Let that pathetic creature earn its own Thorn. It's only fair. It's more than fair. It proves if the creature deserves it or not. Something was wrong. He tried to stop thinking about it.

"Weak, and pathetic," he murmured hastily through labored breath. Such a wretched creature. Missing a piece of itself. Alone and needy.

So very needy ...

"Maybe I will take it," he whispered. He liked the way the words sounded. He wanted to like it.

Night fell. He thought he passed the cave where he had slept. He didn't stop. The bright snow packs began to melt away. It was almost impossible to stay on the trail. He pushed branches blindly from his way. The ground leveled beneath his boots. His whole body wilted at the thought of sitting down. He strained his dulled ears for any sign. It was dumb luck he was able to find his way back to the Lavanya's camp at all.

The only way he knew he had arrived was by the faint light of the embers still smoldering in the fire pit. His hammer shed a weak, flickering glow. He held it before him as he stumbled about, searching. The golden sands glowed as they tumbled from the face of the hammer. Two of the tents had been knocked over. Some clothes lay scattered on the grass. But nothing seemed to have been torn, burnt, or broken.

They're gone.

He choked back a sob.
      He hated himself for it.
"They'd want to know he suffered," he whispered. "—They'd want to know ..."

He kept searching, tearing back canvas, kicking over boxes, and shredding clothing. He hurried back and forth until the grass became matted and littered with shimmering sand.

They'd never leave the sword behind.

He couldn't find it. His Thorn grew even heavier in his hand, creaking and shifting once again. He took the halberd it had become and smashed everything he found. He raked and dashed the wreckage, threshing the debris, hobbling about, bent over and squinting to find a scrap of that dark leather.

They left you to die.

"Cowards!" he shrieked as he stumbled sideways. The darkness echoed back his desperate voice. His throat burned. He couldn't contain himself. "Selfish, horrible—ugly—" He staggered, falling backward. The ground seared his bare palm. He squirmed about in the fire pit. He crawled out of the deep circle of embers.

He slumped to the ground, the fresh shock of the burns gripping his body. He curled up, pulling the staff of the halberd against his body, and wept.

Helpless.
Weak.
P*athetic.*

He didn't understand what was happening. He didn't want to understand. Sometimes he endured it, snarling through gritted teeth. Other times it was too much and he let out a burst of wailing, beating his fist against the ground, tearing at the grass. He didn't get what he wanted. He hated himself for that. He hated how badly he needed it. He let himself scream and cry. He hated himself for that, too.

He froze, his face pulsing with heat, and wet with tears. He held his breath, certain that someone had heard him.

He let you take it.
You know he did.

He crawled away, pulling the halberd with him, dragging his belly over the rugged, dewy grass, flinching at the slightest noise.

You did everything they asked of you,
like a good little boy.

He jerked himself from the ground, lunging into a staggered run.

Now they're coming for you.

Branches slapped his face. The ground pitched, giving out beneath him. His Thorn caught on branches, jerking him about. He fumbled forward, sprinting faster and faster. Then he pushed himself even harder still. The agony of the strain was all that mattered. To ride the pain. To ride the fear. He told himself over and over again,

You deserve it.

You deserve it.

You deserve it.   *You deserve it.*
You deserve it.   *You deserve it.*

You deserve it.

You deserve it.   *You deserve it.*
You deserve it.

You deserve it.
You deserve it.

You deserve it.
You deserve it.

They're going to take everything from you.

2

The young man kicked. He tried to swing his halberd. The hard knock of the wooden staff against a wooden wall. He sat half-way up, his Thorn held out awkwardly before him. His whole body shriveled under the weight of itself. A groan shook free from his lips. He had to lower the halberd. Straw and wooden boards lay beneath his body, as well as a thick layer of golden sand that crunched with every movement. The air tasted musty and confined. Blinding daylight cut between the panels, illuminating the lazy clouds of dust—the paneled walls of the barn—then he remembered. He had found a barn, to hide in from the daylight.

He pulled himself to the corner of the stall, shoving more straw and sand underneath him to support his awkward position, leaning shoulder and head against the wall. His whole body twitched. His breath was rapid and rasping. Something sat in the opposite corner to him. Draped in shadow, it looked like a burlap sack slumped over. A thread of humming wafted through the barn.

Sawdust.

> *They sent him.*

But he wasn't certain it was Sawdust. His body tensed to rise, but he was too frail.

"Did they send you?" he choked out.

The humming seemed to stop. The paneling shuttered from the wind outside, shaking the warped stripes of light painted across the floor. But maybe it wasn't the wind.

"Are they here?" He could barely finish the question, his voice fraying to a feeble whisper.

> *They would come through the front.*
> *No, they know you would think that way.*
> *They're already inside.*

But he wasn't sure they were already inside.

"What are you all waiting for?" he screamed, his voice shaking the barn, using more strength than he had. The humid air was a blanket smothering his sweat-drenched skin. One way into the barn: through the sliding door. He had trapped himself. His attention switched to his Thorn.

> *That's what they came for.*

He should have pulled the halberd to his chest.
But he didn't want to.

Sawdust waited silently in its corner. It seemed they would wait for him to give it up. Or maybe he was just taking a moment he had needed since he left the mountain. Either way, it was over.

He slumped back against the wall with a sigh. His fingernail scratched at the smooth, wooden staff of the halberd. The end was almost a relief.

"I thought I was missing something," he told Sawdust. "I thought ..." he shook his head, "I thought I would find a better part of myself. This Thorn. So I could be less like me, and more like ... Tiger? My lady? Anyone. Anyone besides me. But all this thing has done is make me see myself more clearly.

"I hate myself. I do. But I try ... I want to do my best. But I'm always afraid of making mistakes. I have so many people who love me. I do good things. I think I could do great things. But all I hold onto is my failures. Because I can't change what happened in the past— because I'm scared it'll happen to me again. And it'll be all my fault." He drew in a long, shuddering breath.

"And every moment I hold this *thing* is one more moment where I have to look at all this. To see me. To see how often I give up. How often I give in." He smeared the tears across his face with the back of his arm.

"I'll never be able to do any better than this." He beat his fist against his scar. "Because I'm trapped inside this." He struck himself even harder. The Blackroot flexed. "But that's a lie, right? Just me hating myself? Another thing I'm afraid of?"

He shook his head again. "I can't ... I don't want to see any more. Just make it stop." He threw his Thorn. It rattled and slid, rolling with a clatter across the uneven floorboards, scattering golden sand.

Sawdust didn't move.

The young man's skin grew cold and taut. His Blackroot constricted. The last quiver of light faded away.

"I've done what you wanted," he shrieked, "—Are you happy now?" He pressed his forehead against the paneling, his jaw locked shut.

Sawdust didn't say a word.

It made him think of the willows.

He didn't know why.

~

He sucked in a ragged breath.

He opened his eyes.

Everything was tensed.

He couldn't remember falling asleep. The slices of sunlight had moved, now drawn across the floor from the opposite wall of the barn. He had slept through most of the day and felt all the more exhausted for it.

He stirred.

He had lost something. But what was it?

He looked around the dank and shadowed space. What had he done wrong? Where were the Lavanya? Where was Ymrosch? Sawdust remained seated at the opposite corner, his Thorn lying near its slumped-over form. A scattered trail of golden sand led back to his boots. He flared to feeble life, needing to react somehow, to run, to fight. But then he stopped, his body rigid, his eyes fixed on the halberd. He had given it up.

Of course you gave it up.

His hands retreated into fists, pressing against his stomach. Was he going to leave it with Sawdust? He didn't want it. He could remember that. Could he remember that? It had been a problem from the moment he found it. He couldn't remember exactly why. He knew it would be worse if he picked it up again. Besides, he had made a promise and then broke it.

Just like all the rest.

...

Is that true?

Something was different. Leaving it was the smart thing. The easy thing. Tiger always told him to travel light. And, really, it didn't matter what he had lost if he couldn't remember what it was. Why did that not feel right? Because he hadn't lost it. Whatever it was, he had given it up without a fight. He looked away.

Can I live with that?

He leaned forward, hesitated, and then rolled onto his stomach. He dragged himself along the floorboards, through the golden sand, toward his Thorn. He glanced often to the sliding door, as well as the loft as he shuffled along. His Blackroot readied itself, tightening over his wounds. Arm over arm, his breath drawn as quietly as possible, he crawled the distance.

Keep your promise.

Who cares?
You already failed.

He was lying next to his Thorn, his face near the battered and filthy weapon. The blade and spear point were chipped. The staff had long gashes and caked blood all over it. Someone had been abusing it.

Take it back.

Nothing has changed.
Nothing will ever change.

He took hold of his Thorn, just below the ax-blade.

The light rushed back in.

He looked up to Sawdust. But it wasn't Sawdust. It was a regular sack of something, he couldn't tell what. Disappointment. Confusion.

He rolled onto his back, the halberd held to his chest. It grew heavier as it lay there, pressing down on him.

> *The Lavanya were never here.*
>> *How could Ymrosch get here?*
>> *Are you so arrogant?*
> *How could I've known?*
>>> *Are you so pathetic?*

He lay lifeless until he couldn't contain it any more. He moaned. He shut his eyes tightly. The crush of cluttered thoughts didn't matter, Ymrosch and the rest didn't matter, because he was looking for a way to get rid of his Thorn. Because the power was terrifying. Because the understanding was a nightmare. He was looking for a way to give up. And he knew he wouldn't stop. He didn't know how to stop. It would've been better if he had left it to rot in Ymrosch's belly. But that wasn't the truth. Something inside hoped that wasn't true.

All he could do was lay there, searching the wood-paneled ceiling, seeing nothing at all, trying to breathe, trying to contain everything that had happened, trying to stop trying, and too broken to care about anything at all. The barn reeked of poison and lies, of self-destruction and sabotage. He knew that wasn't true. But he could run away from the barn.

He struggled to his feet, staggering for the door. It clattered as he threw his body against it. He blundered back, collapsing to the ground. The halberd shone brilliantly in his hands. He saw it from the corner of his eye. An effortless understanding. He was doing that. Golden sands rose about him, drifting up into the musty air. There was a hard cracking sound. He lunged through the door. It blasted to splinters in a blaze of emerald light.

He left the crippled barn in a shower of wooden hail. A muddled dusk hung over him. His head was reeling. His body slumped over, fevered with anxiety. The weight of the halberd bent his body crookedly. He had to keep moving. He needed to stop.

The fog of terror faded as night took hold, hiding him, protecting him. choking him. Even so he couldn't stop. A spur of fear needled the back of his skull, driving him on. It didn't matter whether it was true or not. It felt like the only way. He made it the only way.

The Lavanya are right behind me.
Sawdust switched himself out
with an ordinary burlap sack.
Ymrosch could break free of his mountain,
if he really wanted to.
They'll never let you get away with it.

It was like falling forever, the branches racking his body, the blackness of night coming at him too fast to comprehend, only to react. The world was pain. The pain in his knees as he staggered across a paved highway. The pain in his wrist and neck from carrying the halberd. The pain in his arms as they struck rocks and trees that he didn't see coming.

Somewhere along the way they stopped being rocks and trees. They became hard, edged, and stacked somehow. And the sound when he fell against them: dull, flat, and rough, like clay. The air pressed hotly on his chest, his neck, and face. He choked whenever he breathed in, the air dense with soot and a fetid smoke.

He thought he saw shifting rows of dark, shifting pillars, shrouded in the haze of a gray and pink glow. The ground seemed flat, but cluttered with dry brush that hissed when he kicked at it, and snagged at his boots.

He kept blinking. His eyes stung from dryness. There was a sound that he could not place. A soft, low growling, a tickling hiss, and a crackling of some kind. It was everywhere. The heat was suffocating.

They led you here.
They couldn't follow me.
You don't even know where you are.

He knocked into another pillar. He bouncing back, spinning away, choking on another deep breath of something horrific.

"Look out, man."

His Thorn was a battleaxe. He brought it down on the voice. The blade bit deep into dry soil. Golden sand erupted. He had to plant his feet to work it free.

"Hey, hey! Relax!" the voice said, now somewhere behind him. A woman's voice.

Someone real?
One of the Lavanya.
Or someone just like them.

"Thief!" he swung the ax with all his anger. It cleaved a pillar with an hollow cracking noise. More sand poured out. Drawn so close, he finally saw one of the pillars clearly. It was red mortared brick with dry grass growing from the crevasses. It must be a forest of them.

"What have you come for? Say it!" His gauntlet roiled. It bulged. It split open. He struck the bricks to powder, breaking loose his ax. Dazed, swaying, he stared down at his massive, serrated gauntlet, now riddled with fans of curved spikes. He could finally see it:

It wanted to feel the pain.
To feel alive.
It wanted to fight.

"What do you want from me?" Saliva spilled from the corner of his gaping mouth. She wanted his Thorn. She probably didn't know him at all. He just needed her position. It was all the same.

"What's your problem?" she shouted.

He spun about with a wild swing. The ax-blade bounced from striking the hard soil at an angle. The golden sands chimed.

Don't believe her.

"Get it over with!" he bellowed, coughing as he stalked through the smoke, leaning on chimneys as he passed them, wheezing and grimacing.

She'll take something from you.
You don't know that.

"Fight me! Just fight me, you coward!" he screamed over and over again, his voice growing more hoarse and higher in pitch with every guttural breath.

They're all the same.
You can't know that.

The Blackroot rippled across his back, splintering as it swelled, forcing his neck forward, dragging him down and staggering his steps.

He stalked the chimney forest,

dragging his ax behind him,

his breath hoarse,

his eyes blinded by hatred,

and his aching wont for pain and destruction;

it was as though time refused to pass.

3

Something moving to his right. He drove his gauntlet through a chimney. He fell into the crumbling brickwork. Greasy black smoke swallowed him. He stumbled away, falling to ground, retching. Tears poured down his soot-caked face. But he could hear the woman coughing. He wiped his mouth, smearing the spittle and ash. His Blackroot had an idea.

He staggered about, wrecking chimney after chimney, blasting showers of brick in every direction, flooding the fetid air with thick and pungent smoke. He had to stop often, to double over, his hands on his trembling knees, coughing violently. His throat was on fire. His skin felt like it was burning. But she was suffering too. He heard muffled coughing and sniffling somewhere. He had to shut his eyes.

Just as long as she's hurting.

His breath came in short, rapid gasps.
The world was spinning.

Just as long as she feels what I feel.

He finally saw her, between the crooked chimneys, a stocky silhouette doubled over and coughing.

He lumbered toward her. The Blackroot swallowed his other arm in plates and spikes. His muscles strained beneath the weight. His vision blurred. Gaining what speed he could, he charged toward her. He heaved the battle ax above his head with both hands.

Just as long as she dies with me.

The ax fell. She caught the blade. Her other hand stabbed his scar with five finger-points. His armor shattered, exploded, splintered pieces spinning off in every direction.

He collapsed.

Frailty ravaged his body. The hateful heat gnawed at his flesh. The cruel soil scoured his tender skin. He couldn't stop shaking. He held himself. The roar of the fireplaces trampled in his ears. His right hand convulsed with every beat of his heart, the blood gushing from the gaping, pink wounds. It flowed freely out of the drenched scarf-bandage and onto the rutted and dusty ground now littered with glittering sand and Blackroot splinters.

"Don't take it from me," he finally sobbed, barely breathing.

She was bent over again, her hands on her knees. "...Telling me I'm not ready," she muttering hoarsely. "I'll tell you when I'm not-*not* ready. You'll be, like, the first to know. And hey, guess what, I'm all-a-sudden all kinds of ready." A fit of coughing took her.

Everything began to fade.

She came to stand over him.

"I want to keep my promise," he whispered.

"I'm sure you do," she said. She reached down and picked up his Thorn.

~

The first time he woke in a fit of coughing.

Firm green grass lay beneath him.

The air was crisp, the night sky awash with stars.

His injured hand had been cleaned and bandaged with white, soot-stained strips of linen.

His Thorn was still in his other hand, pressed to his chest.

A polished bronze ladybug was marching up a wagging and tenuous blade of grass, right next to his eye.

The second time she was nearby, pacing. A dirty, sleeveless linen tunic. Torn, baggy pants. Rosy skin patched with soot.

His scar itched.

The ax lay on the grass beside him.

The ruby had a long, thin crack, filled with the golden sand. Who had broken it?

He took hold of his ax, pulling it close. Each grain of sand sung as it rolled and bounced off the face of the blades.

His whole body prickled. Every blade of grass under him was burrowing into his flesh.

The wispy, luminous clouds sailed across the endless black sky.

He had never seen them fly so fast before.

Piercing sunlight made him stir. He coughed and shaded his stinging eyes. It was dawn. He could see the chimney forest in the distance, a pitch-black smudge among rolling green hills, crowned with a sprawling brood of thunderheads. He felt the smooth wood of the staff of the ax in his open palm. She hadn't tried to take it from him yet. The Blackroot was already growing back. A few tight plates of carapace gripped his injured hand. The pauldron had come back too, a folding of thin shells binding his shoulder. A small kindness.

"Worried you weren't coming back."

He looked around to find the woman on a rock on the far side of the clearing. She half-grinned at him, this young, stocky athlete with short blond hair and broad, full lips. She sat cross-legged and leaning forward, cradling one arm in the other. It was bandaged, and obviously injured.

He scowled.

An ordinary person.

"Don't, you know, try anything," she said with a wave and a wary chuckle, "—'cause I don't know if I have another one of those in me. Like, if you're gonna keep spazzing out."

A small pile of berries sat beside his head. He couldn't remember the last time he had eaten. He eyed them, sniffing at them from a distance.

"Eat, man," she said. "You gotta be hungry."

She could've killed me in my sleep.

He scrunched his nose. Scooping up the warm, plump fruit, he dragged himself awkwardly to a nearby rock. He eased his back against it, propping up the ax next to him.

She watched the sunrise. A serene calm shone on her face. "Feel any better?"

"No," he croaked. He sniffed the berries more thoroughly before placing a few in his mouth. Delicious. He stared absently at the ground, his mind a rising tangle of all the same old thoughts. "I know you're going to try and take it from me—"

"Hey!" she shouted, cutting him off, "'Thanks, you know, for saving my life or whatever'." Then she answered herself: "'Yeah, no worries, friendly.' 'Oh, and sorry I've been an immaculate tool since the moment we met. What's your name?' 'No problem, my name is Jayne. Wow, thanks for, y'know, treating me like a real-life person—'" She clapped her mouth shut and shook her head wildly. "Seriously, what is your problem?"

"Everything is my problem."

A flurry of blinking. She collapsed into laughter, tried to speak, was overcome by a fit of coughing, and then laughed even harder. It was a throaty and vivacious ruckus.

He tossed the berries away. He glowered at the rising sun.

Jayne tried to catch her breath. "'Everything's my problem?' Are you kidding me?"

"You don't know," he said.

She was silent. He looked to see her watching him with pursed lips and pensive eyes.

"No, actually, I totally do," she said as she climbed down the rock with a grunt. "You're a clenched fist. I know. So am I. But you want to know the difference between you and me?" She stepped toward him, chin pushed forward, jabbing a thumb into her own chest. "I'm trying to do something about it."

He crossed his arms and looked away.

She uttered a noise, something between a growl and a sigh. "Look, man, whatever's going on with you, you're gonna have to figure out there's a big difference between fighting the good fight, and fighting with yourself."

Stupid child.

He decided silence was the most spiteful response.

Jayne gathered his scattered berries, bending over to pick them up one by one. "The only reason I helped you at all was 'cause I know one of your kind." She hesitated. "I owe her." She hurried on, gathering the rest of the fruit. "—And surprise-surprise, you're exactly like her."

She poured the berries into a pile near the young man. Then she stood up, wiping her hands on her pants. The juice almost looked like blood on the linen.

"I have to go. My master'll be worried." She turned and strode away, her stride made awkward by the way she cradled her injured arm.

He stared at the sunrise, uncertain he would ever find the strength to stand again. He grabbed hold of his Thorn and laid it across his lap, the sand spilling from the blades. He traced the grain of the staff with his fingertips.

She could've taken it from him. She could've done anything to him. But all she did was help. What was her angle? Did she know it was broken? Was there something in the berries after all? Was she going to follow him in secret now? But she told him he was only toying with himself.

What a stupid, stupid child.

What does she know? How could she possibly understand? Maybe not yet. But she would learn. In time she'd learn how to lose things. How to be afraid. How to doubt and hate, and feel helpless. He dug his thumbnail into the wood. He couldn't wait for her to fail.

I wish I could watch her fail.

His fingers stopped. It was like hearing his own thoughts for the first time. His jaw flexed. An acrid taste washed over the muscles. It was the feeling that he'd already traveled too many miles down the trail to turn back.

One more failure.
No wonder the willows gave up on me.

It felt too much like the truth.

He slumped over, hiding his face under his arm, no longer able to stand the light.

If only the land would cover him,
to let him sleep forever.

Ian Abdo

4

Velvet grass slid beneath his restless body. Night had come. But a single, cold light shone down on him. Pushing himself upright, he lifted his eyes. The boatman was towering over him. A black, tattered robe hung from his cadaverous frame, the hood pulled low. One of his sallow, anemic hands propped up a staff. A lit lantern hung from its hooked head.

"What are you doing here?" the young man said. But it wasn't his voice. It was a boy's. He looked down to see a boy's hands gripping the grass.

He sat at the center of the circle of willows. Everyone was there with him, encircling him. Bear, deer, fox, and boar hemmed the clearing; squirrel, sloth, blue jay, and owl weighed down every branch. Hummingbird and firefly floated and flitted overhead. Tiger, Python, and Monkey were seated upon their stone dais. His family stood to one side, his lady, his daughter, and his son. Beside them stood the old witch, chin held high, draped in black, white, and blue. Perdue was there too, arrayed in shining, regal attire. So were the giants, Ink and Quill, filthy as ever, and slumped about their raging campfire, watching him over their shoulders. The four Lavanya sat and leaned and crouched on boxes before a canvas tent as though they had practiced their casual poses. Sawdust was seated on the grass like a sack of flour. Coincidence stood next to it, the two of them watching him keenly. General Krejcarek was there, his broad arms crossed. Ymrosch was a hollow, cracked eye peering between the willows. His ice beard had tumbled between the trunks and rolled over the maze of exposed roots. The ashen-haired child was sitting on Ymrosch's beard, his knees up, his elbows on his knees, and his expression smug. Jayne had made it as well, strolling in with a grin. A tall, gaunt and bent man stood at a distance, half-turned away from the crowds, dressed in an immaculate robe of black silk and burlap. His skin was quite pale, his long hair braided, his shadowed face heavy with burden. The distant, sorrowful voice of a violin echoed in the night. There was even more than this. Faces he forgot. Faces he missed. It was everyone he knew. Everyone he would ever know. He wondered where the great willow was.

The boy rose to his feet, flattening his skirt of willow leaves. He turned about, gazing warily at all who were watching him.

"What's going on?" he said.

Silence. That was all that they could offer him. And he knew they couldn't answer him. There should have been something comforting about that—looking across the crowd, every mouth shut firm—something familiar. But he couldn't suffer the silence.

"I found it," he said, turning to his lady. "—I don't have it with me, here, but I took it back." He felt Tiger's gaze. Thinking of all he had done, he shrugged his shoulders, hiding his face from his guardians on their stone dais.

But then he turned, stomping toward Tiger. "I did what I had to do! You weren't there. You didn't see. I did what no one else could!"

Tiger looked down on him, nose held high and glowing amber eyes half-closed. The boy felt even smaller.

"What do you want from me?" he cried out, turning, searching the placid expressions that surrounded him. Everywhere he turned he saw expectation, need, disappointment—so much disappointment in those vacant, absent faces. The grove tilted.

"What am I supposed to be? What am I supposed to do? —Do you even know?" He choked back a sob, shouting even louder, "—Would you even tell me if you did?"

He gasped and rubbed the tears from his reddened face. There was no escape. The grove turned about him, gathering speed.

"What do you want?" He lost his footing and fell to hands and knees. Sucking in a desperate breath, he shrieked, "What do you want from me?"

He slumped to the ground, lying there for a very, very long time. The crush of silence and stillness. Something was not right. He lifted his head. Ymrosch stared back at him.

Ymrosch.
The Bitter One.
The one who gave up
and let a mountain grow over him.

The young man had remembered how it had felt in his presence, the first moment he had entered that icy banquet hall. The stench of something stale, old, and filled with regret. It was as though he was there again, how it saturated his nostrils. But it wasn't Ymrosch. It had never been about Ymrosch. It was his own skin that reeked, that had kept him company since he left the mountain top. That's not true. It had been there for years. And the stench had grown repulsive.

He dragged himself to his feet. "I can't turn out like you," he said, his voice quivering, his lips drawn tight. "I have to do better than you."

He turned to the Lavanya. This was the only place to start, the only way to escape that hollow gaze. He spoke loudly so everyone could hear. He planted his feet, his fists held against his stomach, casting fearful glances back at Ymrosch:

"You didn't take anything from me that I didn't give," he told Ro, because he knew Ymrosch would never do something like that. "The old witch warned me. Twice. I didn't listen. It was all my fault."

He came to the old witch. "You tricked me. You were scared and bitter and lonely. You took it out on a child," he said, like he should've told her years ago.

"But I'm not a child anymore." He almost turned away. But he remembered to say, "—And thank you for making such an amazing daughter."

He cast a glare at General Krejcarek, taking pleasure in the fact that he was dead.

One more glance to Ymrosch.

Finally, he came to stand before the stone dais, before his guardians. He stood a little taller as he looked up at Tiger, his shoulders heavy, his gaze resolute. With arms held open he cried out, "I will never be what you want me to be. And I can't try anymore." He smiled through the tears. "—But I can be simple. I can stop blaming others. I can let go of the past. I can let it be ... let it all be whatever it is, just the way it is."

He nodded compulsively. "So I'm letting go." He looked to his lady. Lines of tears rolled down his cheeks. A deep, heavy breath. His body ached with a hollowness, a kind of weakness. And yet, for the first time in a long, long time, he felt as though he was light enough to carry himself.

He wanted Tiger to say something, or his lady—for anyone to speak to him. But he knew that his own words had to be enough. It had always been this way. It would always be this way.

As he looked around one last time, fully settled in a young man's body, his Thorn in hand, surrounded by silent witnesses, he felt something welling in his chest, tentative and yet strong. It took him a moment to understand the new sensation. There was now enough room in his heart to grow.

He looked to you, his face shadowed with frustration.

Sharp pain rippled up his right arm. The lantern extinguished. Everyone disappeared. The young man was kneeling before his son. A pearl of crimson light floated over them, painting a small circle of red light around them. Another pain shot up his arm. The boy held the young man's forearm in a fierce grip. The boy was drawing the mark of the red tree in his palm.

The young man watched his son plow an index finger through his rough skin, retracing the lines, re-pressing the dots, the skin splitting and shredding beneath his touch, the blood thick and gleaming, oozing out of the gouges. Every touch razed his body, contorting muscle and bone, racing up his arm, and setting his mind on fire. Each time the boy finished the mark he would begin again in earnest, hunching down with hair over his face, tongue pressed between his short, flat teeth, digging his finger deeper, as though he could never quite get it perfect. The young man watched as though from a great distance, drunk with grief.

The boy lifted his head. But it wasn't his son's face. It was too brazen, too eager and alive with anticipation— he saw too much of himself in it. With wide eyes and a crooked smile the boy whispered, "Isn't it exciting?"

5

He dry-retched, fighting to cough up the smoke that clung heavy to the bottom of his lungs. But there was another pang. A piercing pain in his belly. He flopped onto his back, on the grass, with a sharp whine. Digging into the waistband of his skirt, he took hold of something warm and metal. He pulled it free. His eyes focused. He was looking up at the pewter soldier in his hand.

The soldier stared him back, his metal face bent from fear. He said, "Go home."

He snatched up the battleaxe and dragged himself to his feet, throwing himself forward, stomping down the grassy hill. After the outburst he slowed himself to a hobbled jog. The strength from his restless sleep wouldn't last long. Brisk air cooled his stiff skin. Sluggish muscles refused to wake.

You'll never make it.

It had taken many days to travel to Ymrosch's mountain. He wasn't even sure he was going in the right direction.

They're better off without you.

His body cried to stop, to give up and lie down. He dug in, pushing harder. He hated how weak he felt. Every frantic breath shredded his throat.

Ymrosch could still be following you.
The Lavanya could be watching.
You can't keep this pace for long.

It took everything he had to ignore it all and fight on.

The sun broke the horizon. He found a gravel road and veered onto it. The packed earth and stone made it easier to gain traction. He switched the ax to his other hand. There was no relief. The rhythmic hiss of golden sand striking the gravel chased his heels. He pushed even harder still. His lungs threatened to collapse. His thighs burned. The sounds of crushed and scattered gravel from beneath his staggered footsteps.

Move faster.
Move, you pathetic child.
Just get through it.
They don't need you.
Push through the pain.
Wouldn't make a difference if you made it.
Let go.

The road diverged ahead. A great ash tree stood at the fork. He strained to keep his chin up, to focus as he approached. The right path sailed over rich, rolling hills, lit by the morning sun. The left path descended into the violet haze of the waning night. One would lead him home. The other wouldn't.

You're going to pick wrong.
You always do.
You'll never make it.

He faltered, tripping over his boots. He crashed to the stony path, sliding and rolling to a feeble stop.

A gentle breeze.
The honey-sweet scent of daphne.
The quiescence of a rolling, grassy plain.

His arms and legs stung where flesh had been shredded through gravel. It was a kind of relief, laying beneath that towering ash, wrapped in the anger of pain, squinting up at the swaying branches.

He tried not to think about what might be happening to the grove. He tried not to think about another troop of scavengers attacking. Or something even worse. Maybe they were too many for his lady. Maybe she was injured. Maybe they captured her. Maybe they killed her. Maybe the grove was burning to the ground. Maybe they were all dead. And he let it happen. He left them alone because of a selfish need. Was it a need at all? They were dying. It was his fault. And now he was lying at a fork in the road in the middle of nowhere with nothing to show for it but a broken body, bloody gashes, and a heavy, heavy battle ax held tightly in his fist.

Let go.
You're all alone.

He squeezed his eyes shut. But all he could see was Ymrosch glaring back at him. He thrashed lamely about. Dust and pebbles clung to fresh wounds.

"I can't end up like you," he whimpered over and over again. Every time he said it he believed himself a little less. He tried to sit up, but he couldn't find the strength.

Let go.

He stopped struggling.

He lay back down, staring up at the gently swaying ash, frowning.

He had said those words in his dream.

"Let go," he whispered. It tasted wrong, to say it out loud. But there was something else there, just below the surface.

He tried it again. "Let go?"

It had made sense, before. But some things are easier in dreams. He gripped the staff of his ax. The delicate squeal of splitting glass.

"What am I letting go?" he asked himself, because the young witch wasn't there. Because his guardians couldn't help him. Because no one could do this for him. And somehow, he knew.

This has to happen here.
Now.

"I'm letting go of everything. All my fears. All my hate. All my pain. Everything that's happened, and everything that might happen. I can't end up like him."

They sounded like empty words. They felt empty. But it was enough to begin:

He rose to his feet, chose a path, and marched on. Deep, deliberate breaths. One foot in front of the other. Too much time had been wasted lying on the road, lost inside. He let that go.

A walk became a jog. He listened to the rhythmic crunch of his boots on the gravel, and the pulsing sound of the golden sand hitting gravel. A fit of coughing exhausted him. He staggered. None of this changed the fact that something terrible might be happening to his family. He let that go too.

A jog became a run. He pushed too hard. When his lungs burned and his body bent forward in helpless frustration, he let it go, slowing his pace, doing what he could with what he had.

Carefully, diligently, he found his way,

> Like the young witch threaded needles,
> Like Monkey spun a tale,
> Like Python unraveled a riddle,
> Like Tiger trained a student.

His legs grew lighter. His breath found its own pace. He crossed a stream that he had seen before. His legs grew weightless. The sweat rolled easily down his temples. Somewhere along the way his Thorn had become a dagger again. He set it into the waistband of his skirt. A stand of pines looked familiar. He was getting closer. He let go of waiting for the next thought to rise. He just ran. And when the next thought came— as it always did—he let that go as well.

He broke through a crowd of old gray oaks, into the Lavanya's meadow, the sun blazing overhead.

Yes, his heart chanted.

Yes, his mind sang.

Yes, his body roared.

He sprinted through, plunging back into the forest. Tree and rock and stream flashed by, coils of dust, dead leaves, and golden sand rising in his wake.

~

He paused at a creek hidden in the shadow of a cliff face. His body ached, weary but sturdy, his skin slick with sweat. He knelt down to take a drink of the crisp waters.

The hairs on his neck rose. He looked up. A black dog was staring down at him from the cliff's edge. He pulled his Thorn from his waistband.

Ymrosch sent him.

No,

It was probably the Lavanya.
Sawdust still wants the pewter soldier.

The dagger burst forth, extending into a short sword. The dog didn't move. A quartet of crickets were chirping in the tall grass. He frowned.

He stood upright, letting his sword hand drop to his side. Grains of sand danced down the blade, showering the ground.

Don't trust it.

I don't have to.

The dog stared at him, unblinking. Its limp, mangy hair waved in the breeze, its split ears raised.

He waited, stifling a cough.

It watched.

He walked away, keeping an eye on his watcher until there was enough distance between them. The sword became a dagger. He returned it to his waistband as he turned and ran on.

He glanced back a short time later. The black dog was behind him, seated, watching him jog away.

He stopped to remove the boots, kneeling to unlace the first one. The black dog was sitting at a distance behind him. Another one had joined it. They were nearly identical; the same opalescent gaze, the same long limbs. He noticed each wore a metal collar, thick and crudely wrought. He squinted at them.

He sat down to unlace the second boot. He never saw them move—never saw them blink. Their gaze was indifferent, as though it was nothing more than a job. The Blackroot gauntlet had retaken his whole hand and forearm, so he used the claws to slash the laces in a single motion. He tossed the boots away and ran on, lighter and faster.

Soon there were four.

By the time he could see the ridge of his valley on the horizon there were seven following him.

The sun had begun descending in the west, washing the sky in a blood-red haze. The ridge seemed already darkly shadowed. The scattered, taller trees were all the greenery that remained. He quickened his pace.

When he drew close, having wound his way through the last stand of pines, he slowed to a stop. The hillside wasn't shadowed. It was covered in black dogs. They sat packed shoulder to shoulder, every eye fixed on the young man. His hand touched his Thorn's handle. Behind him, twelve dogs sat in a semi-circle. But a narrow path had been left open, winding up the hillside all the way to the top of the ridge.

He marched up the path. Every pointed, moist snout turned, following him as he climbed. The evening air reeked of mold, and something rotten, as though he was surrounded by a field of corpses. He tried not to think about what he might find. He tried not to think about his dead children, his burning home, and even worse horrors that he could scarcely imagine. He didn't know how to let that go.

The lines of black dogs on the ridge above faced away from him, looking down the length of the valley. He couldn't see what they were looking at.

He used his hands at the end, sliding, clawing and clambering up the final stretch of loose soil and bald rocks. A blustering wind met him at the top, taking him in its sweltering embrace, swirling his sand all around him. He hurried to the edge. Waves of billowing, stone-gray smoke filled the valley, obscuring almost everything. A muddled crown of hungry, deep-red flames was consuming the grove.

Black dogs lined the opposite ridge. They too were looking away. He only had a moment to see where they had all set their eyes. An army was marching into the valley. He couldn't see where their ranks ended. Curtains of dust rose from their masses. The sides of the valley were set ablaze as they chewed at the land, crawling toward the grove.

He threw himself from the ridge, flying down the hillside and into the valley of smoke.

Part IV

~

1

He sprinted through the burning grove, vaulting over the fallen trees, splashing through dried and muddied creeks. Gray smoke pressed against his singed flesh. Thick, glowing amber ash swirled about him. Tears poured from his squinting eyes. His throat constricted with every labored cough. The horrified cries of the animals filled the grove. Sometimes they were hard to distinguish from the sounds of the charging flames. He had to trust his memory to guide him, his arms reaching forward as he raced blindly toward the circle. He couldn't feel his daughter anywhere, but his lady was with the great willow.

He stumbled to his knees, a sob bursting from his lips. But there was no time. He pushed himself to his feet and ran on. He had been so certain for all these years the willows had abandoned him. But now he knew they had still been there, watching over him, listening to him. He knew this because he no longer felt them at all. Were they looking after his daughter now?

He drew near the center of the grove. White and red lights grew before him, swirling and slicing through the dense smoke. He heard the chaos of breaking branches, upturning earth, and the cracking of electricity. He crashed at full-speed into some vine-like bushes. They held him back. Pushing and fighting through the foliage, he realized the branches were familiar to him. It was a fallen willow tree. He struggled furiously, breaking through, and staggered into the clearing.

Half of the willows lay fallen, broken on the ashen ground. The rest were on fire, flicking red tongues lapping ravenously up the blackened bark. Gray sunlight poured down through the vast hole in the canopy left by the fallen trees, filtering darkly through the tempest of blackened smoke. The great willow writhed and twisted in hateful agony. The deep cracks of its charred bark spewed white sparks and flame. All its leaves had been burned away. Its gaunt, whip-like branches tore through the circle, flaying and scorching everything it touched. The remaining willows had braided their branches with many of the great willow's, restraining its movement as best they could in a tangled, radiating web. But the great willow had set these braids aflame, igniting leaves and bark. It jerked its captors back and forth until they cracked and split beneath the abuse. Even its sprawling roots wrestled desperately against the other willows, thrusting up great mounds of stone and soil. With a final lurch backward, it tore open a gaping hole in its trunk. And a primal, deafening moan shook the air.

The young man fell to his knees with a jarring stop. His blood-shot eyes grew wide as the tears streamed down his hot and ashen cheeks. The battle rang in his ears. He could feel the willows wailing in his heart, and the great willow's voice was among them. It was an singular, endless cry of pain, of terror and despair, and overwhelming, unquenchable grief.

Tiger clung to the side of the great willow, tearing out mouthfuls of wood with his powerful jaws. Many branches had descended on him, wrapping around his waist and neck, strangling him, trying to burn him and pry him loose. But his massive claws were extended, dug deep into the wood, and every muscle flexed to a sharp definition beneath his fur. His purple flames swirled around him, haloing his head and lashing out from his many swinging tails. The red tree's fire could not consume him.

The wolf darted back and forth across the circle, ricocheting off tree trunks and rock faces. She was a deft blur of black and yellow whipping through the whirlwind of fiery willow branches that battered everything in sight. Like a bolts of lightning she shattered some of the branches that held Tiger, then launched away before the rest could reach her. But the great tree burst forth even more branches to take their place.

The wolf was at his side. The swelling sensation of electricity in the air. The potent smell of burnt hair and blood. Her fur felt wiry and scorched when his hand absently found her neck. She was shaking. Her feelings flooded him, a staggering wave of desperation and anger. Her words cut deeply:

The willow took our son.

The young man rose. He marched toward the great tree. The wolf came alive again, striking at the limbs that held Tiger, and evading the fiery tempest that engulfed the grove.

"Give me my son!" he roared, wiping the ashen-tears from his cheeks.

The flames rose hotter and brighter. The tree's grotesque mouth strained even wider. The primal moan intensified, causing the air to warp and the ground to shake. Willow branches flashed past his arms and head.

"My son, now!" His voice could barely rival the roiling devastation. Flaming branches jabbed at the ground around his feet like javelins. The roots undulated, rolling away from his path.

Why wouldn't they touch him? Was it because he was scarred by a red tree? This wasn't about him. The tree had been poisoned by Man. Could he take it back? He gripped his Thorn's handle in his waistband. The light kindled inside. He had to try.

"Can I take this from you?" he cried out, searching the red tree for a sign, any trace of the old willow that had watched over him his whole life. Smoldering, serpentine branches loomed overhead, surrounding him, poised to strike and yet hesitant. The jagged, splintered mouth of the great willow twitched, closing slightly, and then opening again.

No, he couldn't take it away. No one could take away his own scar. It was hopeless. He drew his Thorn.

A branch pierced his pauldron, driving him back. He dug his feet into the ground. He grabbed hold of the branch, grinding himself to a halt. A cloud of gray debris and golden sand swirled around him. His eyes flared with verdant fire. The wound from the red tree had been the most excruciating pain of his life. This was nothing.

He lifted the dagger high above his head with a cry. It burst forth, growing into a splitting maul. He hacked off the branch. The spear-like end in his pauldron burst into crackling green flames. He marched forth. The host of branches fell on him as a manic swarm. He deflected them with his gauntlet and maul. He chopped off the ones that pierced him, or wrenched them free. Splinters of charred bark rained down as the wolf bolted overhead, whittling away at the swarm. His pace quickened.

The great tree pulled the other willows inward using their entwined branches, bending them low with a punishing strength. Crimson sap poured from its riven bark, washing down its broad and twisted trunk; it ignited with dark fire as soon as it touched the blistering air. Rage and agony was all great willow had for him, and it was without end. His heart shuddered under the weight of it all. But he let it go, and kept fighting.

A massive bundle of woven branches battered the young man's body. He spun through the air. He hit one of the willows trunks and fell to the wrecked and rocky ground. His head ached from the endless onslaught of sight and sound and heat. He strained to focus his eyes. He tried to suck the air back into his lungs. Tiger was on the bundle of branches, digging his claws and teeth in. Billows of dust and ash and purple flame filled the air as he tore away at it, wrestling it to the ground, wrenching it free from the red tree's trunk. The young man rose again, hobbled but upright. He marched for the red tree, striking down the branches that came for him.

Vengeful arcs of electricity leaped about him as the wolf bolted across the clearing. Purple flames encircled him in ravenous waves as Tiger rampaged. The young man's firestorm had grown, now billowing around him, now a dazzling fury of white and green lights. The glittering sand hung weightless in the air, like all the stars in the night sky.

Even so, he could feel the nauseating heat of the tree, its singular rage focused on him, beating against him with wave after wave of revulsion. A rush of weakness rippled through him. But all this was happening because of the poison. So he took a breath and let go of it one last time.

He was standing at the foot of the great willow. The maul became a dagger as he set it in his waistband. He fixed his steel gaze on the tree, grounding himself, gathering together the flecks of his will, and raised his hand, palm up. The tree opened its trembling mouth, with desperate fits of resistance, until the bottom jaw reached the roots, making something like a gateway. It shuddered to a stop. He stepped inside. Before he could look back at his lady the gateway clapped shut.

2

All was dark. All was silent. The chaos and carnage of the circle had been shut out so quickly he felt as though he had been dropped into the emptiness. He could sense that he was in a large area. Cool, humid air shifted about him. The sounds of drawing in a raspy, quivering breath, and then letting it back out. He lifted his hand, which he couldn't see. He wasn't sure why his light had failed. Maybe he just needed a moment. There was so little of him left. A broken body. A reeling mind. A hollow heart. It made it easier. He had only one thing to depend on. His hand came to rest on his Thorn. A dagger bleeding sand. He hesitated. Then he gripped its handle, flooding the space with green light. The sand began to pour again.

He stood at the top of a well, as wide as the great willow itself. Roots of every shape and size hung just above his head. Thin currents of smoke hung in the air. He stood at the top of a staircase of knotted roots which spiraled endlessly downward, beyond the reach of his light. He laid bare fingertips against the wall. The wood felt warm but supple, and still alive. He pressed his forehead against it.

"Don't make me do it," he begged.

He cantered down the stairs, cautiously and quickly. He descended into the tree for a long time with nothing but the sound of his ragged breath, the padding of his calloused feet against the root stairs, and the pattering of sand. He wondered if he would find his son, and if he was still alive. He wondered if his daughter was alive, wherever she was. He wondered what was happening above; if the great willow kept fighting once he had entered; if the army had arrived yet. He wondered if the willows still protected his children. He wondered when he would have to kill the tree. He wondered if his Thorn still had the power to kill the great willow. He didn't know how to give that up. He quickening his pace.

He reached the bottom of the staircase and stood, winded, with one foot resting on the last step. He looked out into nothing, his light unable to pierce the darkness. A shuffling came from beneath the stairs. He walked around to find a small cage shoved underneath, made of many woven roots. He crouched down. Inside lay black and red fabric, pale, bruised skin, and black hair. It was his son, curled up and holding his head.

"My boy," he gasped and reached for him. The roots parted before his fingertips, retreating, dilating to a wide opening. His son didn't move. His hand stopped short of touching a pale knee.

"Are you okay? Are you hurt?" He seemed to be breathing. It could've been a trick of the light.

"Please, please speak to me."

He couldn't touch him, not without knowing for sure. But he wasn't moving.

"It was not my fault," the boy finally mumbled from beneath his arm.

The young man stifled a sob, a smile on his dry and cracked lips. "Come here."

"I was working on a variation of a newer sign, and I was in a fresh section of tunnel, so I—" The boy fell quiet.

The young man readjusted his crouched position with a grunt, waiting for his son to speak again. His hips ached. His knees felt swollen. Anger started to rise, muddling the moment of relief. His Blackroot readjusted itself. A subtle, boiling anger. His son shifted slightly, though he never sat up, or even showed his face—his son, so smart, and always full of confidence. His son, who had carved a sign into the great willow.

"No," was all he could utter.

His body crumpled forward. His fists and knees pressed into the ground. His head hung low. It was the only explanation, and the only reason for the dream about his son. He suffered the nausea from mounting waves of anger. The Blackroot groaned as it swelled across his back.

"Isn't it exciting?" his son had said in the dream. Of course he would say that.

He took an exasperated breath as he sat up. His son hadn't moved.

Arrogant.
Spoiled.
Stubborn.
No time.
Let it go.

"Are you hurt?" he finally whispered.
"No."
"Good."

"Use every opportunity," she always told him. He unclenched his fists. He had to let it go. But his son didn't deserve it.

"What did you do?"

"It was not my fault."

"Son, I need to know what happened," he pressed. "The willow is very sick. Will you help me?"

"No," his son murmured, burying his face even deeper.

Forcing himself to his feet, he marched off, putting space between them. He threw back his head, choking out a laugh. His light flickered and dimmed.

"I don't know what to do here," he called back more harshly that he meant to. "I think you hurt the willow. But it doesn't matter right now. Something isn't right. I want to make it right, with you." He shook out his gauntlet as he sucked in a hissing breath. "—But for some reason you won't talk to me. I don't know if you're afraid, or if you're just being stubborn. Maybe you feel guilty. I just don't know. But this has to be fixed. You can stay here, or you can join me. But I'm going to do something about this."

His son lay still, his face covered.

He wanted to reach out to him, but his son wouldn't show his face. He wanted to scream at him, but that wouldn't change a thing. There was a awful taste in his mouth. He turned and walked away.

Can you let it go?

He stopped himself.

He stood there for longer than he should have.

He shook his head.

"I'll be back. Son, I have to do this and then I'll come to get you. I promise."

He didn't wait for the response that would never come.

~

He was running through the vast cavern. But the darkness surrounded him, an impenetrable shroud that followed him no matter where he turned. A thin and feeble line of golden sand lay in his footprints. He stumbled, slowing to a limp jog, peering into the impossible blackness. He lost track of the staircase somewhere behind him, beyond the trail of shimmering sand that faded into the black. The only sound was the soft hush of his feet through the cool, cool soil, and the pitiless silence. It must have been larger than the grove itself. He started to wonder if it had walls.

His son had carved only one symbol, hopefully. But he was uncertain where to begin looking for it. He was afraid for his lady. He was afraid for his daughter. His home was burning to the ground. And an army marched above him somewhere. He was afraid of his own thoughts, so he stared out into the darkness, every sense strained. The infinite space grew all the more heavy with despair, and the ache of loneliness. He wasn't sure if he could feel the great willow anymore. Or maybe this was how the willow felt? That thought troubled him even more. He hurried on.

Finally, a wall appeared before him, blossoming as it entered his circle of light. He slowed. There was a small tunnel in the wall, framed by tangles of roots. As he approached it he saw another tunnel nearby. He looked the opposite way. More tunnels, unevenly spaced, and of different sizes. Had Python known about this place? He stopped. His scar itched below the surface where he couldn't scratch it. He was never going to find his son's carving. But he closed his eyes and took hold of his Thorn's handle.

You can't do this.

Maybe I can feel the poison?
And the roots might glow red?

He lifted his gauntlet, reaching for the fire, the poison, and the hatred. He opened his heart, searching for everything that he feared. His clawed fingertips shivered. Something was there. He could feel it immediately, like a thunderstorm roiling on the horizon. It was always easy to find. It seeped in, saturating his blood and bones. He shook his head. He shifted his feet. Then he walked toward it.

He passed tunnel after tunnel. The feeling grew, swelling in his chest, staining the overwhelming darkness in front of him.

What will I find?

You can't fix this.
You can't even fix yourself.

Let it go.

He had to stop, to lean against the root-lined wall, to hang his head. He tried to quiet his mind with a deep breath and a deeper sigh. It didn't do much.

A red light blossomed before him.

"You are close," his son said.

The young man turned to see his boy standing at a distance, his arms folded, his chin tucked.

A wince of a smile crossed the young man's face. He nodded. "I can feel it."

The pearl of light soared away, coming to a stop over a not too distant tunnel. Some of the roots that framed this tunnel were blackened, shriveled, and the ground was tilled, as though two objects had been dragged out from there recently, taken in two different directions.

With his son watching, he strode to the tunnel. It was small enough that he had to drop to his hands and knees to enter. The air inside was warm, arid, and tinged with rot. He had only crawled for a handful of stifled breaths before realizing that his son's light had faded. He looked over his shoulder. The boy still stood at the entrance of the tunnel, little more than a pair of pale, skinny legs to his eyes. He sat down, leaning his back against the side wall.

"Son?" he said.

"Something is wrong in there," his son whispered, shifting his footing.

A spur of anger, a rush of guilt, but all he could do was glare at his son's dirty knees. They were shaking. He was scared. Of course he was scared.

This fragile boy had never faced a red tree, never known fear towards his uncle Perdue, never crawled out of the belly of a mountain. And he never wanted his son to go through anything like that.

His gaze fell to the ground. He rested his hand on the handle of his Thorn. The tickling sound of splitting glass. No matter how smart his son was, he was only a child. And however terrible the consequences, he had made a child's mistake.

You're treating him like he's you.
You're scared.
You're running out of time.
You're failing him.

He sat silent, a fist pressed against his scar, enduring his thoughts. When he could bring himself to speak, his voice was tender and full of restraint.

"Yes, it's scary in here. I've got to go inside, to try and fix what's wrong. I understand if you can't follow me. But if you want to come with me, I'll keep you safe. You and I can figure this out together."

It only took a moment's contemplation before the boy shuffled up to the tunnel and crawled inside, his light trailing behind. "This does not appear to be a well-thought out plan," he mumbled.

The young man let out a breathless chuckle. "We work with what we got," he said, and brushed the hair from his son's face. "Let me know if you come up with a better one, okay?"

"Of course."

3

The tunnel was long and straight. He could see all the way to the chamber at the end, and the pulsing red lights waiting for him there. The ground beneath his hands buckled a couple times. Showers of dirt rained down on him. A grinding, growling sound swelled as they came closer. He crawled over charred and smoking roots. His son stifled a cough.

"You can go back, if you want," he said.

"I know."

The air grew suffocating, full of the sweet tang of rot. Sweat rolled down his face and arms. His hair clung to the sides of his face. Fiery lights colored the tunnel in swirling dark red and orange. The ground rumbled beneath him. He wiped his brow with the back of his dirty forearm, casting worrisome glances as he worked his way forward.

His son was right. It was barely a plan at all. Could he use his Thorn to hack off the mark? Would that make a difference? How was cutting off a piece of the willow any different than carving a sign into it? He clenched his jaw. The mark had already poisoned the willow. Maybe it was too late. It was out of control, like a wounded animal blinded by pain. And it would kill them all unless he stopped it. He couldn't catch his breath.

He came to the end of the tunnel and looked down into the great chamber below. The lights were flashing and flaring from a wretched heart of roots. A searing, boiling symbol was carved on it. It writhed about, pulsating, bleeding dark fire and poison that gushed out, falling into a pool far below. It was suspended in the center of the chamber, bound by an array of knotted, wiry roots that shivered with every violent spasm of that hateful heart, rattling the walls, shaking loose sheets of soil, and churning the turbulent clouds of crimson dust. Tunnels were scattered about the chamber. The ground shifted beneath his hands and knees. He had no way to know what he would find, but this was too much. Too much pain. Too much agony.

"Go back," he said. But the grinding sounds had become so much louder. "Son, go back," he shouted. The tunnel collapsed, giving out beneath him. Dirt blinded him. It filled his ears. He couldn't stop rolling. His son knocked against him. His body slowed to a stop at the bottom of the chamber. He thrashed about, rising from the dirt and rocks. A branch exploded from the heart, piercing his pauldron, driving him back down, deep into the loose soil, plunging him into the darkness and heat, pinning him there. A thrumming deafened him. He screamed in his struggle. Ashen soil filling his mouth. The packed earth hampering his movement. Strength drained from his broken body. He had to kill the willow.

A timid, muffled voice pierced the thrumming. He could barely hear it. His son, terrified, maybe even hurt. He was able to reach his Thorn. He pull it free. A branch sliced through the soil, missing his side. He worked his arms up, raising them above the branch, positioning the dagger. It burst forth, growing into a quarter staff. He wrapped his legs around it and braced it again the branch with both hands, twisting his body as hard as he could. Another branch came for him, this one grazing his thigh. He let out a whimper and a shudder, straining every muscle, pressing through the mire of pain. The branch began to crack. With a final moan he broke it. The rest of the branch plummeted deep into the ground beside him. Taking hold of it, he dragged himself free, gasping as his head broke the surface. The lights and sounds bombarded him. He spat and coughed. He shook the dirt from his face and hair.

His son was crying. He lay face down, squirming in the deep soil, surrounded by javelin-like branches. One had pierced his leg, pinning him there. Blood was soaking through his dirt-caked skirt.

The willow was going to die.

The young man scrambled toward his son. He stumbled through the deep soil along the bank of the dark and fiery pool. He pulled the wooden stake from his pauldron. More spear-like branches pummeled the earth around him, throwing clouds of soil into the air. He struck a couple of them with the his Blackroot fist, shattering them to splinters. The quarterstaff burst into green flame, incinerating, revealing a katana within. He lifted the blade above his head with both hands. He planted his feet and sliced clean through the stock of branches that held his son.

He dropped his sword and fell to his knees among the slender stumps. His son was clawing at the loose soil, moaning hoarsely into the dirt as he struggled.

"I'm here," he said, and clutched the branch that pinned his son's leg. The wood ignited, hungry, emerald flames chewing away at the charred wood. The fire inside him dwindled from the effort.

He felt it before he saw it. He lifted his gauntlet open-palmed toward the heart. The spear-like branch pierced through the chitinous plates. It drove his hand back and to the side. But he gripped the spear, holding it up, straining to keep it from striking the soil and pinning him down.

He looked back. The thin stump turned to ash in his other hand, freeing his son's leg.

The heart thrashed wildly, poison and fire spewed across the tortured chamber. The pool below it roiled, spitting and churning. The bank's edge rose, creeping toward the young man. His light was fading. He reached for his sword. The heart had gathered its hideous strength. Another spear flew at them.

He raised his bare hand. Blackroot flashed up his arm. The branch pierced the armored palm, driving that arm back as well. He bellowed, straining forward, holding onto the branches. The heart drove him backwards. But he dug into the earth with knees and toes, bracing himself in front of his son. His light died. His body was failing.

You failed.
You're a failure.
You have to kill it.
Or it'll kill everything it touches.
Just like you.

His body shook, slipping backwards against the branches' spiteful strength. This was all his fault. Everything was burning because of him.

Because he trusted the old witch.

Because he left the grove.

Because he wanted the Lavanya.

Because he woke the young witch.

Because the boy was his son.

Because of all of his weaknesses, and fears, and doubts, and failures. None of this would've happened if he had never been born. He didn't know what was true anymore. But it was impossible to hold it inside anymore.

He opened his cracked and bleeding lips. A wretched sound came out. It grew louder and louder until it was a hateful, bitter wail. His grief was unending. He sucked in another gasping breath, wailing even louder still, unable to get it all out.

A hand touched his chest. He fell silent. His eyes snapped open. No one was there. He blinked in the mire of his exhaustion, still wrestling against the heart, still buffeted by withering lights and brutal sound. He looked to his clawed hands, pierced through. He gripped the branches even more tightly, giving himself over to the strength, searching the pain, losing himself in the touch:

An uneasy stillness filled the half-circle of willows. Only the crackle and snapping of small, scattered fires could be heard. Layers of thick, white smoke hung in the air. The young witch stood before the great and listless willow. Tiger stood behind her, keeping a close watch. Her eyes were closed, her head bowed forward, her hands placed on the scorched and blackened bark. She was speaking gently. It was the language of her Secret. She had spoken it to him and their children for many years. He had never known a name to call her elegant and exotic words until now. He never understood it. But he loved listening to her speak it; words of compassion, words of kindness, of warmth, and courage. He knew the sound of those words well.

He returned to himself, his beaten body shaking, straining against the branches. He looked up at the wretched heart, his eyes bloodshot and shimmering.

It's too late.

"Let me carry it with you," he said softly. He didn't have to scream. He didn't have to fight the deafening fury in that dust-choked chamber. It heard him.

The heart pumped sluggishly, erratically.

It's going to kill you.

"I'm here. Let me carry it with you."

The heart slumped to a stop. Poison and fire dribbled from its crevasses. Its light faded, its skin grew hard, and it shook as though it was suffocating.

A shriek broke across the chamber, a horrendous, unbridled pain, gripping everything with its unnatural force. A great, crooked spear exploded from the heart, driving itself through the young man's scar. He dug in deeper, bracing himself against the onslaught, and found his footing. He craned his neck back to see that the spear tip had not reached his son. Then he set his sight wholly on the heart.

You can't fix this.

"I can't fix this," he whispered, leaning in, his voice shuddering under the effort. "I can't change anything. But I can carry it with you."

The heart's strength wavered, surging in fits and starts. One of the branches in his hand jerked back, shriveling as it slipped free of him, retreating back into the heart. He reached for his Thorn. It leaped from the ground, flying to his hand. A thunderous cracking noise rang out. Fire burst from every wound, from his eyes and mouth, a flood of dazzling lights washed over the chamber, steeling his bones.

He saw why he needed to leave the grove. He saw why he needed to suffer. He saw why he needed to fail. Golden sand rose, filling the air, swirling and sweeping up around him. It was all for this moment. It was for the willow. The grief and gratitude rose, mingling, saturating him, until they were a single, overwhelming power.

The wretched heart lurched back, ripping the branch free from his other hand. It pulled at the great and crooked spear. But he sunk his claws in, gripping it with all his strength, keeping it in his scar. The heart dragged him forward with a lurch, struggling to free itself. He plunged the katana deep into the ground, anchoring himself. The heart writhed, struggling with what remained of its waning, desperate strength.

"Nothing will be the same after this," he whispered, "but it's not the end. It's … another beginning. It may be hard, and you may lose your way. You're going to lose parts of yourself, but you will never be lost, because I'm here."

The heart strained, a frail burst of agony and denial. But he refused to give up. They kept coming, words he had not known would be there:

"You're going to fail, but that doesn't make you a failure. You're going to want to give up, and I'll help you figure out the things worth giving up. And you may think these scars are all that's left of you, but you don't need them to be whole. You don't need them to be strong." His voice faltered, his shining eyes having grown bleary, his heart pounding in his chest. Those last words were a lie. He couldn't spare the strength to face that just yet.

Nothing happened right away.

The young man waited, uncertain of what else to do, what else to say. His own fire settled, though he kept his light alive.

The heart shrank slowly, smoldering.

Its pulse fell shallow and even.

He readjusted as best he could, his lower-back aching in the movement.

Eventually the heart stopped fighting him altogether. He breathed a sigh of relief, collapsing to his knees. But he only had a moment.

"I gotta go. You know I do." He released his claws.

The branch shriveled, sliding out of his scar. It broke free of the heart, falling to the ground, one end and then the other, kicking up the fine soil into a cloud. Blackroot wove around his open wound. It didn't help the fresh, throbbing pain.

He took up his Thorn. It turned back into a dagger. The ironwood handle was now scorched and pale. The leaf blade was chipped. It was smeared with blood and ash. The ruby shone, a low, pulsing light from deep within. But its face was scarred by three deep cracks, and many hairline fractures covered the rest of it. The golden sands flowed freely from those cracks, pouring out onto the lap of his torn and weathered skirt. He let out a shuddering sigh.

You did this.

You're killing it.
That's what you do.

He closed his eyes, stifling a sob.

An army is waiting for you.

He sheathed his Thorn in his waistband, rose, and looked to his son. The boy sat against the slope of the chamber, his finger tracing something in the loose soil. He couldn't find the strength to be angry. With great discomfort, he knelt down before him. "Are you alright?"

"Yes."

"Your leg?"

"I cannot feel it."

He didn't know why he didn't break at those words. Something inside braced him. He laid his hand on his Thorn. He let go, searching deeper, through the guilt, past the grief, reaching beyond himself. It was easy to do it for his boy. His back straightened. His gaze softened. He nodded and said, "That's normal."

His son was stoic as always. But it was clear that he was shaken, sinking into his thoughts. The young man laid his hand on his son's uninjured leg. "It'll be alright. We'll figure it out," he promised, pointing to his own scar like a promise.

"We can figure it out," the boy repeated. He would not look him in the eye.

The young man gathered up his son with a grunt, the boy's arms around his neck, his legs around his torso. He looked over the tunnels that were scattered about the chamber and then shuffled off toward the closest one.

"We'll have a long talk after this."

His son didn't respond, but he held his father tighter, pressing his face into the crook of his neck.

Ian Abdo

4

Neither spoke as they climbed the spiral root staircase. The young man's light was dim, his breath raw and labored. His lower back ached. The tops of his thighs burned as they approached the top. His son readjusted his grip often. The young man wondered when his son had gotten so heavy. He often opened his mouth to speak, to comfort, to teach, to punish. But no words came out. One ear was always listening to the pattering of sand as it rolled down the steps behind them, too many to count. His sluggish mind struggled to keep count anyways. Finally, at the top of the stairs, he gestured halfheartedly. The mouth-gate opened before them.

Tiger turned his head as they appeared. The young witch had been waiting, leaning forward, her fists pressed to her chest, her dirt-smeared face bent with worry.

"Good man," Tiger said. "What happened?"

"Where's our daughter?" the young man said as he walked down into the half-circle.

"She is safe with Monkey," the young witch said.

He set their son carefully on a mound of charred roots and then shuffled away. He found a root-cradled stone and slumped down with his back against it. A moan escaped his lips.

The young witch knelt before her son. The boy sat so very still, his eyes downcast, his shoulders hunched forward. She reached for him, hesitated, and then ran her fingers through his filthy, greasy, matted hair. She leaned in, resting her forehead against his.

"You need a wash," she said.

He leaned in. He looked like he could cry.

The young man cupped the dagger in his trembling hands, his palms pressed against the ruby. But the sands persisted, trickling and spilling out between his fingers and into his lap. The willow was a red tree now. It could still hurt them. It could still burn the grove down. Healing would take so much time, if the army didn't destroy their home, if they don't all die in the war to come, if his dagger didn't break during the battle.

If,

if,

if...

"What happened?" Tiger said again.

"Please, just give me a moment."

The young witch rose, approached the young man and knelt before him, taking him in her arms. He dropped his Thorn and held her as tightly as his strength would allow.

"Thank you," he heard her whisper.

He let her go when she pulled away. Her soot-stained arms were laced with fresh blood. "No ... Oh, no ..." He looked with despair at his hands and arms, still covered in the plates and spikes of Blackroot. He shot upright, looking to his son. He too had been marked with threads of blood, now smeared and darkened from their journey through the willow.

He tried to apologize. But the young witch took his face in her hands and kissed him fiercely. He wanted to hold her. He gripped the dead soil instead. Her tears felt hot against his cheeks, and salty to his lips. She sat upright again, sniffling, drawing her hair from her face. She had heard his thoughts.

"We must go," she said.

He nodded. "We gotta go."

"I will bind his wounds," she said. "Python?" she called out as she returned to her son.

"I am here," Python responded, appearing from what little underbrush still remained. The young witch spoke to the guardian as she tended to their son's leg. There was something comforting about seeing Python in that moment.

"I will not ask again," Tiger said, his voice rising.

"I'm sorry, Tiger." The young man said. He took up his Thorn and dragging himself to his feet. "The willow was marked, poisoned, but it—" he struggled to find the right words, "—it remembered itself. It's with us again."

"Who is responsible for this?" Tiger said, his fangs showing.

He hesitated. "My son marked the tree, but I am the one responsible."

Tiger snapped his head about, eyeing the boy.

"Please, there's no time. An army's marching into the valley. They're burning everything."

Tiger looked back to him, his lips curled back and his face twisted in disbelief. He lowered his head. He turned and ambled away, his singed and ashen fur rising. He slashed at the ground frenetically, shredding loose curtains of soil as he roared, spewing out billowing flames and furious rage.

Python and the young witch stopped.

The young man stood between him and his son, Thorn in hand.

When Tiger had spent himself he stood silent among his carnage, the black curls of smoke turning slowly about his stoic frame. A final, settling exhale burst from his nostrils, stirring the smoke.

The young man hadn't noticed that the stone dais had been broken in the battle.

"The willows can no longer protect the grove," said Tiger. "Only we three remain."

"Done," the young witch told her son. "Go with Python. She will keep you safe." He obeyed, rising unsteadily to his feet. It seemed as though he was going to say something to his father. But the moment passed. She spoke to him softly. She kissed him on the top of his head. Then the boy and Python disappeared into the brush.

"I am ready," the young witch said, tightening her utility belt on her hips.

"I knew today was a good day to die," Tiger said with a sardonic grin.

"Are you able to fight?" she asked the young man.

He nodded, pressing his palm to his scar as he flexed his Blackroot pauldron. They stood where the flesh-colored flower once grew. Only a handful of charred and curled roots remained beneath their feet, now dusted with ash and sand. He eventually found his voice: "We'll do what needs to be done."

Her brow creased slightly, as though he had said something unexpected. But he was already moving.

The young man led the way as they sprinted through the lifeless, smoke-strewn grove, between bent and burned trees, over fallen debris and still-smoldering underbrush. No one spoke, though a plan would need to be decided on.

Only one thought circled his heavy head:

>   *Don't fail them.*
>   *Don't fail them.*
>   *Don't fail them.*

There was no hatred in the words, only fear and slow-turning doubt.

Ian Abdo

Part V

~

1

The young man drew the final curtain of willow branches aside and the three stepped out into the valley. The sky was blotted out by a thick haze of dust mingling with the smoke. Gray ash fell like fragile snow. The sounds of the army reverberated across the valley; the hiss, crunch, and thud of thousands of feet trampling the ground. The fat, grinding cry of revving motorcycles, calling to each other from across the masses. The ceaseless chatter of rustling fabrics, furs, metal, and flesh as they jostled and pressed forward. And the bellowing hoard of voices, a smearing of fevered, indistinguishable noises. The air reeked of engine exhaust, the heat of sweat, body odor, grease, the bitter tang of crushed vegetation, and the lingering, mordant smoke. It was difficult to discern how close they were.

"I will fly ahead and kill the leader," the young witch said.

"Be careful," The young man said.

"Be merciless," Tiger said.

"Promise," she said. She sprinted ahead. She threw herself into the air, disappearing into a burst of black and gold feathers, a momentary, spherical constellation. It sucked back in on itself to form a Black-Gilded Finch, ducking and darting off into the haze. It was incredible to watch every time.

The young man was waiting on Tiger. He only just realized it. His guardian sat beside him, his chin held high, his eyes half-closed and yet piercing, his breath a deep and guttural purr. Tiger licked his lips. Heat pulsed from his great body. That was his world, waiting for him just beyond the veil of smoke. The young man stretched his neck and shook out his legs, trying to relax his shifting, creaking Blackroot.

"I see you found it." Tiger remarked. "I had no doubt."

The young man pulled his Thorn from the waist of his skirt. "Yes I did, with luck ... and plenty of help."

"Not that." Tiger turned his steady eye on the young man. "To commit to a choice, and embrace the consequences. These are the weapons of the warrior."

He couldn't meet Tiger's gaze. It wasn't like before. He returned the dagger to his waistband. Staring straight ahead, into the haze, all he could say was, "I'm trying."

"—and there is the measure of a man."

It was unsettling. The young man was happy to hear what Tiger was sharing with him. But he no longer needed it. He couldn't remember why it used to be so important.

"I am hungry," Tiger said, rising. "Ride with me into battle?"

The special honor was not lost on him. The young man grinned at his guardian now coming alive with anticipation. "It would be rude to not welcome our guests."

"Yes, exactly!" Tiger laughed heartily. His eyes flared like stoked embers, sparks rising from the tongues of flames that began to ripple over his fur.

The young man lit his own fire as he took hold of Tiger's mane, vaulting himself up onto his guardian's sleek and muscular back. With deathly silence they tore through the caustic haze, tilling the ground beneath them with his claws, slinging red and green fire and dark soil into waves in their wake. The young man held on tightly, tucking down to keep himself from falling off. The mephitic wind howled in his ears and slapped about his hair and skirt.

To embrace the consequences.

The words rushed like a shiver up his body. He's always had to suffer from his mistakes. Why would Tiger think that has changed? How could that ever change? The wind abused his exposed skin. His guardian was speeding beneath him. But it seemed as though the world stood still.

To embrace the consequences.

Blackroot swelled over his shoulders and rippled down his arms, fresh spikes fanning out like fingers. It was as if it had been waiting for this moment ever since he had seen the great tree on fire. He reached for his Thorn. He hesitated. It was chipped and filthy. It was cracked and leeching sand. Fitful streams of it twisted and scattered to the rivers of wind and fire behind them. He left his Thorn in his waistband.

Blood drummed in his ears. His clawed gauntlet wrapped around one of the spikes on his opposite pauldron, near his scar. His breath quickened. He wrenched it loose like a tooth. It shuddered, shifted, and tumefied in his grip, spikes and saw-ridges jutted out as it grew into a hideous mace. He held it, trembling yet ready at his side, his body arched forward, his eye fixed on the swirling, shapeless haze before him.

Let them come.

A wall of bodies. The raw and heinous torrent of clashing metal, flesh, and hateful, primal cries. With only the slightest rocking from the first impact, Tiger powered on, grinding through the endless ocean of soldiers. The heat of his body only intensified, a blazing, fuming fire that heaved from his body with every swiping lunge, every limb torn loose, every wave of enemies sent flying. The masses were washed in boiled blood and viscera.

The fat crack of scattered gunfire. The tireless, fitful cries of motorcycle engines. The stench of singed leather and hair mixed with body odor, hot metal, and ash. Grasping hands and wheeling weapons. Dented, filthy, mismatched armor. Twisted, screeching, ghoulish faces. Blood mixed with oil splattered against his body. A mewling bray boomed over the valley.

The young man hacked blindly to the right and left, bludgeoning faces and mauling limbs, whatever might leap from the maelstrom. His other gauntlet held Tiger's mane in an iron grip to keep from falling during the sharp turns and the breakneck speed of his strikes. It was hard to breathe.

Just like the chimney forest.

More than once his mace shattered to sharp splinters. Then he would throw his Blackroot gauntlet wildly, beating down on the masses that surrounded them. The waves of frantic bodies rushed without end from the acrimonious haze, throwing themselves against Tiger. The young man would grab a soldier by the jaw or neck, dig his claws deep into flesh, and drag them choking and screaming through the battlefield. Then he would take hold of a spike of Blackroot, rip loose another hideous mace, and start again.

A shadow fell over them. The muddy ground erupted. The world spun, first the brown of the army, then the gray of the hazy sky, then the brown again. The young man, Tiger, and the surrounding hoard had been scattered to the wind. Bodies and armor clapped together, bouncing off each other. Tiger might've crushed him in the fall. The young man marked the horizon. He lunged off his guardian.

It seemed as though he would never land.

He plunged into the army, leather and metal pulverizing him until he was dragged to a halt. But nothing was still. The press of bodies on all sides, blades and blunt objects slapping and sliding against him. There was nothing to hold onto, nothing to orient himself.

He lashed out. His Blackroot complied. He didn't know what it was doing. Blackroot surged and swelled. He let it happen. Gnashing and grunting. The hollow, hungry cracking of Blackroot. A guttural scream. He couldn't tell the difference between blood, sweat, and mud. The heat of fresh cuts pulsed across what little bare skin remained. Lurching strikes. Swinging limbs. He kept waiting for ground to meet him. But there were only helmets, chests, and tangles of shifting legs of every side. He tried to reach his head up. He couldn't find the surface. Side to side they threw him, sometimes in a gradual sinking, sometimes in a fitful shove.

He kept struggling, clawing at everything, stabbing with anything the Blackroot gave him. The chitinous armor creaked across his back and down his legs. His arms felt heavy from injuries, and the busy carapace that crept along his skin, binding fresh wounds, folding over itself, weight upon weight. His vision rimmed red. He dropped his Blackroot weapon. He pulled in, tucking up his legs, and covering his head with his arms.

Just like in the chimney forest.
You're losing yourself.

His foot struck solid ground. He swung his arms, pushing and lunging until both feet were firmly planted. His hand found his Thorn.

Better to die a Man,
than survive a Monster.

He left his Thorn in his waistband.

A scream flew from his lips. Every muscle seized with hateful steel. Scales and whipping spines of Blackroot erupted from his body, exploding out in every direction, skewering soldiers, shredding armor, and piercing flesh and bone. The Blackroot latticework had pinned a broad compass of the army in a moment of suspended horror. Those that could speak, wailed. Those that could move, squirmed. The latticework cracked, and then shattered. The dead and injured soldiers dropped with a single, wet, crunching sound. The young man fell to his knees. He was gasping through grit teeth, swaying, struggling to keep from falling over.

Exactly like the chimney forest.

More soldiers closed in around him. It was a cruel and lonely moment that spread out for eternity:

Tumbling golden sand stuck
to the churned mud.

His Blackroot creaked as he shifted.
The hot, metallic stench of the battlefield
soaked his skin.

Let it go.

Above the helms and blades, Tiger, wreathed in fire, clung high on the back of a towering, savage minotaur. It was like nothing the young man had ever seen before. It was covered in grimy hair, torn and sodden rags, and bound in many collars and chains, all dripping grease and clotting blood. It had three sets of horns in its head, set like a crown. Countless long spears radiated from it back and shoulders like porcupine quills, and they flagged back and forth with every spastic motion of the beast. Soldiers all around it held its chains taut like leashes, while more soldiers spurred it forward with many more spears at its back. A mewling bray came from its snarling, foaming mouth. Twisting and lurching about, the minotaur toppled to its knees, shaking wildly, struggling to get a hold of Tiger.

Let it go.

The young man staggered to his feet, already scrambling, and then sprinting at the minotaur. He charged through soldiers, throwing them aside and stepping over others. Some plates and piece of Blackroot sloughed from his back and legs, giving him more speed.

Tiger's jaws were locked onto the beast's thick neck, purple fire flooding from between his fangs, pouring down the minotaur's hairy body. Riflemen all around were firing at the guardian. Plumes of fur and flame erupted from Tiger's body where the bullets pierced muscle.

The young man swept through the masses, pulling a spear from the ground as he approached.

The minotaur found a grip on the nape of Tiger's neck and tore him loose, beating his body against the ground. It stumbled to its feet, swinging the guardian back and forth, crushing and scattering any soldier it could reach. Dark, glistening blood spurted and gushed from its neck in the labor, soaking hair, flesh, and metal. The beast was still on fire. Tiger clawed at the minotaur's face, twisting free from its grip.

The young man flew at the minotaur. The spear struck at its heart, the iron tip shattering against the blackened blood. The beast staggered. The staff of the spear snapped. He slapped against the minotaur's meaty shoulder, spinning away, skipping over the army like a stone before sinking into the hoard. The harsh crunch of restless bodies against his Blackroot. The hiss and screech of a hundred voices in his ears.

I can't.
There are too many of them.

He let go of his fear.

What can I do?
What is left?
My Thorn.
My broken Thorn.

He let go of his thoughts.

Charging, purple flames surrounded him. Tiger broke through the chaos. He was larger somehow. The young man took hold of his fur, dragging himself onto his guardian's great back as he trampled past. Tiger pivoted hard, tearing his way back toward the stumbling minotaur.

"Cursed Ironblood," Tiger roared. He could feel the words through his guardian's back more than he could hear them over the battlefield. "Aim for the neck wound. Downward thrust."

"Got it," he screamed back. He pulled out his Thorn. This wasn't right. Even so, he leaped to his feet, steadying himself with one hand still clutching Tiger's fur. His Thorn's ruby pulsed sluggishly, the sand pouring out, dancing on the wind.

Don't break just yet.

He launched himself high into the air. Through the haze, the hoards were like a field of wild grass far beneath him, ebbing and rolling in waves. Soldiers throughout the ranks were carrying tall banners. Dark shadows threaded the army, rapid blurs that seemed to dart beneath the surface, slipping between their legs.

Tiger was already attacking, his searing fangs locked deep in the minotaur's forearm, wrenching it back and forth, dragging the beast off balance.

In a flash of fire and light the young man forged his Thorn into a spear, his eyes fixed on the bright pink wound in the beast's neck where Tiger had injured it. There was a better way.

He swung early, sending himself spinning, shifting his direction. The spear shattered to brilliant pieces revealing a katana within. He landed in an explosion of scattering mud, soldiers, lost weaponry, broken metal links, and golden sand. He had broken one of the minotaur's chains. The baleful creature notice. With its freed hand it took hold of a soldier by the head and lifted him high, beating him into the ground. It threshed all of its tormentors.

"TIGER! LET GO!" the young man shouted as he wrestled thought the pandemonium, working his way to

Ian Abdo

the next chain. That one was shattered as well. It took another shout to get his guardian's attention but Tiger released the beast, bounding away.

A shadow flew past him, low to the ground. He saw more of them circling the minotaur, hidden among the troops. Soldiers began to drop.

Many soldiers turned their attention on the rampaging beast as it tilled the battlefield. In this moment the young man was finally able to take a breath and look over the valley, or what little the haze would reveal to him:

Much of the army was termite soldiers, dressed in their make-shift armor and rusted weaponry, jostling and scrambling over each other. But there were goblins among their ranks, smaller, hunched and hairy creatures with large noses and little, hollow eyes. Their big, knuckly hands carried axes, hooks, and hatchets. He saw slow-moving motorcycles of different makes and models scattered about, and orxy riders as well. A handful of massive, lumbering giants towered over the soldiers. And there were more minotaurs in the distance. Many tall black banners were held high above the helms and blades, each one a long, worn and tattered length of fabric bearing a white symbol: an isosceles trapezoid made of four crude hash marks. Altogether it was an endless, churning sea that dissipated out into the haze. He worried about his lady.

A soldier charged at him.
He struck him down.

Through the hurried, shifting bodies he saw a black dog standing over a dead soldier, eating. He searched the field again and saw black dogs everywhere, chasing down the wounded, the cowardly, and the many fallen, and consuming them all.

Another soldier came, a goblin.
He put him down as well.

Tiger was without mercy. He had grown in size, muscles bulging beneath sliced and scourged fur. Ravaging, ravenous purple fire was a swirling about him, swallowing soldiers whole. It seemed as though he had more eyes, and many rows of teeth. A brilliant crown of flame sat upon his head, and his many tails were longer, coiled with wicked flame as they whipped about. A pack of black dogs followed his wide, charred, and bloodied trail.

A pack of black dogs scattered from a certain area to his right. The air swelled. Rising. Expanding. The world turned white. There was no sound, but the ground shuddered under the impact. He staggered backwards, his arms raised, his blinded eyes shut. There was nothing for several stifled breaths.

His sight was the first to return. The young witch lay in the middle of the battlefield, torn, white-singed dress and bloodied, pale skin. The ground was scarred with a blackened, root-like pattern radiating from where she lay. Bodies had been set aflame about her, sheets and bits of torn clothing drifted through the thick and misty air. The hoards rushed at her. He scrambled toward her, calling for Tiger though he could barely hear his own voice. Tiger was already charging in, sweeping up the first batch of soldiers in a wave of crackling flame. The young man slid to a stop next to his lady. He dragged her back toward the grove. She tried to speak. He couldn't hear her thoughts.

She clutched the Blackroot of his arm weakly. "Krejcarek is alive. You must kill him."

Ian Abdo

Ice snaked through his veins.

"We have to go," he screamed at Tiger. "Can you hold them back?" His voice sounded thin and distant to his pummeled ears.

Tiger, robed in heaving fire, took only a moment to look over his shoulder. One of his many red hot eyes had been gouged out. His countless rows of fangs shone brightly despite the layers of boiled blood and flesh that clung to them.

"At last," the young man read on his guardian's lips. "You little ones were holding me back." Then Tiger indulged himself.

The young witch was already writhing on the ground, kicking at the ash and slinging mud, her marred and haggard body twisting as she transformed.

The young man stood over her, cutting down the piteous few that crawled past Tiger. Far quicker than he expected, a wolf the size of a horse rose next him. Her fur of black, white, and yellow crackled with electricity. He barely took hold of her fur, hoisting himself up onto her back, before she bolted away.

They charged down to the side of the valley, parallel to the ever-advancing hoards. They scrambled up the steep valley wall before veering right to run alongside the army, speeding their way deeper into the ranks toward the general.

2

The wolf carried them deep into the army. The slope of the valley was uneven, with swaths of loose soil and scree to hamper her speed, and yet she maneuvered the trees and bushes effortlessly. They passed rows upon rows of soldiers. They were without end. The chewing sound of their boot-steps was tireless and deafening. Occasionally a motorcycle- or orxy-rider noticed the two, but she was too sprightly for them to do anything about it. The young man began to feel the smoke heavy in his lungs, a distressing, itching sensation. His throat and nostrils burned with every breath. The wolf staggered a couple of times on some loose gravel, but each time she regained her footing, charging forward once more. He could feel the sting and fatigue in her labored breathing.

We should rest soon, he thought.

But she couldn't hear him.

Despite having transformed, he found blood beneath her fur. There was something off about her scent, when he could smell her.

She staggered a few more times along the slopes before slowing to a jog. He slid from her back, matching her pace as they wound her way up to a small, secluded overlook. The wolf collapsed to the ground. He was at her side, holding her as she trembled and struggled to return to a witch.

"It's okay. It's alright," he whispered the words over and over again.

When it was over, she lay very still.

"I need a moment," she whispered, her breath quick and shallow.

"I'm not going anywhere."

She was much older now, with thinning skin and sweeps of silver in her brittle hair. Her bones felt fragile. He breathed her in deeply, searching her over. The pungent, acrid taste of smoke filled his nostrils. But this smoke was heavier, greasy, and reeking of rotten lemons. The cooling, metallic scent of blood. And something else, something elusive, like green apples, or pine needles. Sometimes she winced or shifted in exasperated discomfort. The air swelled with fits of electricity when she did.

Something was wrong. Something he couldn't see.

There was less of her somehow.

He tried to make her comfortable. He readjusted his arms carefully. He re-positioned himself to help keep her back straight. She was coated in a hot, greasy film. Dirt, ash, and blood was everywhere. Her utility belt was torn. Some of the pouches were missing. The side of her dress was soaked, glistening from the blood. It was saturating the top of his skirt. Her left calf was injured too, caked in a thick mud and fine dust.

You're supposed to patch me up, he thought, unable to hide his frustration and utter helplessness from her.

But she couldn't hear his thoughts.

"What do I do?" he whispered so softly. "Just tell me what to do."

Her face was even more pallid than normal. Heavy beads of sweat covered her forehead and cheeks. She was trying to slow down her breathing. He laid her down gently, piling up dirt and golden sand beneath her head and neck.

She could barely speak. "A pair ... long tweezers ... right-hip pouch."

He leaned over her, finding the pouch still intact. He took out the tweezers.

"Bullet ... in my side ... Get it out."

He hesitated, looking at the blood-soaked dress that clutched her body. The tear in the fabric was small. He couldn't see the bullet wound through all the blood.

"Here." She offered her hand. But his hand was a fist locked in spiked plates and scales of chitinous Blackroot.

He unclenched his fist. He wrung his hand out behind him. After much effort one plate fell off, and then another. It took time and taxing concentration to give them up. His arm ached from the effort. Eventually, only a band of Blackroot remained, binding the hole in his hand left by the great tree.

He laid that gnarled and ruined hand on his lady's stomach. She placed hers on top of his. He could feel her once more.

No thoughts were needed.

Relief.

Together they endured the pain and discomfort as he pushed the tweezers into her side. Though her face remained stoic, her body spasmed and shifted as they searched.

They found the bullet. With some fumbling, they took hold of it, and drew it from her side. It was smaller than it had felt inside of her. It filled the air with the warmth and flavor of her body and the overwhelming, hollow stench of rotten green apples. He could see through the dark and viscus blood; intricate symbols had been carved on it. He threw it away.

> *The wound must be closed*, she told him.
> *Front right-side pouch. Yarrow and Goldenrod.*
> *Chew it before applying.*

He leaned over her. The pouch was missing. It had been torn off. She reached for a different pouch, one with bandages. It had been lost as well.

He sat back, letting go of her hand.

He couldn't think straight.

Hopeless.

She was staring up into the haze. A tear rolled down the side of her face.

"Show it to me," she whispered.

He shook his head, utterly lost. "It doesn't matter."

"I want to at least see you."

Pointless.

But she had asked.

He knelt over her. He drew his Thorn and held it up for her to see.

She examined it. Her eyes were clouded with tears. Her pulse was still racing. He could see it in her neck. She nodded slightly, compulsively. "There you are."

He looked at it again. But now he could see it through her eyes. His Thorn, so comfortable in his grip, as though it belonged there. With her it was no longer a weapon. It was no longer a problem, nor something to hate, nor something to fear. He didn't need to understand it. Nor did he need to fear misunderstanding it. It was no longer something he was afraid to lose. Whatever it was, whatever would come of it, it was simply a part of him.

She winced. Some of the golden sand had spilled onto her wound. She sucked in a hissing breath at the discomfort. She grabbed his wrist. They both felt it. It wasn't hurting her. It was cleansing. Her eyes were bright when they met his. She had been hopeful, but unsure if it was even possible. Now there was no doubt.

He held the dagger's ruby over her wound, spilling the golden sand onto her side. It stuck to the blood, piling up, covering the wound. She arched her back in pain.

His Thorn knew what to do next. He sheathed it and then pressed his hand against young witch's side, over the sand and the blood. The Blackroot sloughed from that hand as green and white fire consumed it. Silken, emerald flames lapped up her body, flicking and twisting into the air. She gripped his other hand, her nails digging in. Her face trembled. His light shone on her.

> Their pain was one. And all of his pain crashed in on himself, his failures and victories boiling up, sweeping in, his whole, harrowing journey now returning home with him. His foolishness, his courage, his recklessness, his determination. All that he had seen, all that he had refused to see, and all that he had come to understand—all made real, now that she was there. It was nothing like he had remembered it to be. All he could do was endured it with her.

"Yes, it is done," she gasped.

He pulled away his hand, quenching the fire in a tight fist.

"Your leg?" he insisted, his fist shaking.

"It is fine," she sighed. "Bullet passed through."

He dragged himself to his feet and staggered to the edge of the overlook. He searched the haze of the valley and felt even smaller still.

"I'm sorry," he said, turning back to her. "I should've been here. I should've been better than ... how I've been." Blackroot crept up his neck. He pulled his fists against his stomach. He wanted to hate himself. He wanted to give that up.

"Come to me," she said.

"Come to me," she repeated, her voice weaker this time.

He returned to her, kneeling down.

She took his hand and placed it gently against her tear-shaped scar, saying, "I am not sorry."

She was older now, exhausted, filthy with blood and grease and dirt, girded by some hidden power.

> This gracious mother,
> his ally,
> his warrior,
> his healer,
> his lover,
> and his friend.

He finally believed her.

He pulled the pewter soldier from his waistband. Cradling her hand, he laid it in her palm.

He nodded and said, "I'm not sorry."

He started to believe himself too.

"Kiss me, my brave one."

He obeyed, smiling as he knelt down to touch her lips. She pressed her other hand to his cheek. It was trembling.

"I just need a moment."

He held her in his arms.

~

The army churned on, the countless, raw, and relentless cries of warcraft rang throughout the valley.

The young man readjusted a couple of times, his knees and back complaining. Golden sand pooled around them. It hissed softly when they disturbed it.

"Not yet," she said.

He eventually settled against a rock, his lady's back and head resting on his body. He laid his head back, staring out into the haze.

Tremors crept along the ground.

He hoped Tiger wasn't dead. Or maybe he hoped Tiger had died quickly? No, he'd be too stubborn for that. He'd burn the valley down before letting them take him.

His grove could already be gone.
He didn't know where his children were.
Krejcarek was here. He had done all of this.
The thought stewed in his troubled mind.

~

The young witch stirred. She reached back. He took her hand. She squeezed it.

"Almost ready," she said.

But he had been waiting too long.

"What did he take from you?" He spoke the words as calmly and quietly as he could.

She didn't respond.

She tilted her head. "You can see it now?"

"What?"

"You can see it now." This time it was a statement.

"What did he take?"

"He did not take anything. His snipers shot me, twice ... One of them I deserved. But he would not know how to take something from me."

"I don't—" he began, but the young witch persisted:

"I knew I had felt it, earlier, but I did not know how far you had come."

"I don't understand," he sighed.

"Yes. Yes, you do."

She presented her shapely hand, placing thumb to middle finger. She snapped, throwing a fit of electricity.

"My mother, myself, Tiger, your willow, and you; we all have different magic. But it all requires the same cost. Life." She took his hand once more, laying it on her chest. Her fingers were hot and subtly vibrating. "We exchange future years to manifest power now."

No.

He tried not to think of all the wondrous and terrifying things he had seen her do—things she's done her whole life.

No.

He tried to not think of all Tiger was doing right now, to survive, and to keep the grove alive.

Not this.

He tried to not think about his son.

"Please," was all he could utter. "No. That can't ..."

She pulled on his hand, holding him tightly, pulling him back to her.

"It has been crippling at times, yes, and other times quite liberating. But I finally came to accept this Law of Author. I came to embrace it, through watching my mother, and watching you. You have always understood this, whether you liked it or not."

He took two long and difficult breaths, his chest shuddering. There was no way to deny it. He wish he could. He hated himself for that. But he let it go, laid his cheek on his lady's hair, and whispered, "Everything has a price."

"Everything has a price," she repeated.

"I don't like it."

She made a gentle noise of understanding. "That is the crux, is it not? The life is spent regardless. So we are left with two choices. To grieve the law, or get creative."

It was difficult to speak, but when he did, his voice was certain. "We're gonna get creative."

She shrugged. "That is the way I was leaning."

He kissed her head, chuckling despite himself.

"I am ready."

The young man carefully lifted her up, sliding out from underneath. She grunted from the effort, scooting backward to lean against the rock. The ground was shaking, a low, very slow, and subtle pulse. Evening was coming, the haze of the sky growing darker and even more muddled.

He knelt beside her. "What happened?"

"Krejcarek was ready for me. His whole strategy was designed to kill a witch. He rides an Elder Tarasque."

He didn't know which question to ask first. He started with the last one:

"How?" he said.

"Yes, it barely fits in the valley. He sits on the crest of its shell in a great, spiked, rod iron dome."

"—which protects him from your lightning."

"Precisely. The dome has nine iron arms that run along the shell, reaching out in every direction. These iron arms are lined with bonfires burning piles of Jimsonweed, Bitter Nightshade, and Mistletoe."

"The heavy smoke I smelled on you," he added.

"Wicked alchemy. Troublesome for sight and evil for the heart. The iron arms connect the dome to nine towers. Each of those nine towers holds stacks of cages; each cage holds a Drekavac. At the top of each tower is perched a Hagen Sniper, also protected in a cage."

He shook his head, not understanding.

"Drekavac are little screamers. Their voices disorient, making it nearly impossible for anyone to concentrate. Krejcarek spurred them to a frenzy by running a hammer along his dome, which disturbs their cages—which is connected through the iron arms.

"The Hagen are kin-slayers, honorless assassins. Their eyesight is peerless. They were using hexan bullets coated with Azalea's Nectar, if I had to guess." Her explanation left her slightly winded. She was clearly perturbed.

Krejcarek is trying to kill my lady.

He let it go.

It took a moment for him to let it go.

"You know, after a while it just sounds like you're making excuses."

He almost got her to smile.

"How does he control the army?" he asked.

"I am uncertain. Perhaps he does not. Perhaps he simply funneled the mob into the valley. Regardless, he must be stopped."

"But, what can I do? If you can't stop him—"

"He underestimates you."

He didn't know how far his mind had wandered until she touched him. He came back, finding her hand in his, along with a black strip of fabric.

She gestured around her mouth. "For the smoke."

Loose soil and rocks poured down the valley wall. The ground thrummed.

"He is near."

The young man stood up and turned to look, tucking the fabric into the waistband of his skirt.

A heavy shadow, as wide as the valley itself, swept onto the overlook. The Tarasque was a goliath, unmoving mountain to them, obscured by smoke and haze. The only clue to its forward movement was the deep, reverberation that shook the ground with every footstep, and the space between them was vast. He realized she had chosen this place. They could more easily reach the Tarasque from here.

"We can leave still," she said. A simple statement. "We can give him the grove."

He shot back a look. The Blackroot began coiling and reaching down his arms once more, snapping and creaking as it did its work.

"It had to be said."

He didn't answer her.

Some part of it must have knocked into the valley wall, causing heavy debris and rocks to fall in great sheets down the sides of the overlook.

"Do you have any ideas?"

"Yeah," he said, returning to her. "I'm gonna walk up and stab him in the head."

The young witch looked up at him. "Okay."

He helped her to her feet.

"I will wait for my opening." Her dark eyes flashed golden. "Ready?"

"Ready."

The two locked wrists. They sprinted in opposite directions, turning two full circles, gaining momentum. She twisted with a cry, letting go, slinging him high into the haze of night toward the Tarasque.

Ian Abdo

3

The young man scrambled along the lip of the Tarasque's massive tortoise shell. He used his claws and toes to keep himself from falling as he hurried, circling towards the great creature's head. His dry, burning eyes leaked a steady stream of tears. It was difficult to breathe through the thick fabric of the mask—but the heavy smoke clung to him, and a hot, oily film coated every inch of exposed skin—so he kept the mask on. He could feel the constant shifting and pulsing of the creature beneath his feet, and the rumble of every catastrophic footstep. He had extinguished his light; a useless tool in the smoke. It was impossible to see more than a couple dozen yards in front of him through the blackened haze. Faint and distant fires dotted the horizon to his left, little more than vague smudges of deep red, vaguely outlining the curve of the broad and vast shell he was running along.

He often peered up into the smear of darkness, watching for any signs. He thought he passed as least one tower, its obscured shape rising and fading into the night. He wouldn't be able to see the Hagen before they took their first shot. He scampered on, low and swift as possible.

The churning, chattering of the army was quieter up here. But it was inescapable, needling incessantly at his ears. He found himself humming one of Monkey's silly songs.

> Stinky breath,
> From stinky bugs
> And sticky hands,
> Who needs a hug?

His lady had coated the inside of the mask with peppermint, filling his nose and lungs with a clean, refreshing sensation with every breath. He hoped his children were safe. He needed them to be.

He was uncertain how long it took, but he came to a goliath, leathery outcropping, jutting out from beneath the lip of the shell. He assumed it was its neck, shifting back and forth ponderously, part of the grand gait of the creature as it lumbered forward.

He turned, sprinting up the steep slope of the shell toward the center of the Tarasque's back. He passed several curved spikes, taller than himself; a natural defense scattered across the back of this mammoth creature. The bonfires grew brighter, spreading out into a discernible pattern as he drew near, though still dull and obscured by the great distance and haze. The rough, uneven shell beneath his toes was filthy, covered in fine ash and dust. He ran until his arms were slick with sweat. His skirt flapped against his thighs.

The shadowy outline of a tower appeared to his left. He sank even lower, crawling to the tower, his eyes wide, his throat raw and aggravated despite the mask.

At last he was crouched beneath one of the nine towers. It was a crude and crooked thing, made of some kind of thick metal girders and square bolts, as wide as both his arms outstretched. It appeared to have been driven deep into the Tarasque's shell. Blood had hardened around its base, clustered like dry sap. One of the tall black banners hung from the tower, the same fabric bearing the same white symbol: an isosceles trapezoid made of four crude hash marks. Circular cages clung to the tower like grapes on a vine, though they didn't start appearing until quite high up the structure. He thought he could hear gentle mewing coming from them, along with the quiet, cold clatter of loose bolts and bindings.

The tower was bolted and welded to a wide, waist-high wall—one of the iron arms, he assumed—that ran up toward the center, the crest of the Tarasque's back. Huge, shallow, metal bowls were bolted to the top of that iron arm at an even distance, the bonfires within them crackling ravenously, heaving out their noxious, pitch black smoke. He could see two other faint lines of bonfires on either side of the curved horizon, all three of them meeting darkly at some higher, distant point. A trail to his enemy.

With a bit of exploration he found the tower was stabilized by four support cables, connected high on the tower, pulled taut in four different directions. Each one had been drilled into the face of the shell. Standing next to one of the cable's anchor, he pulled out his Thorn.

"Time to make an entrance," he whispered to it. In a stroke, the dagger became a splitting maul. The cable was cut, whipping away with a metallic cry. The mewlings from the tower grew louder. A couple of sharp shrieks took the air. A short jog, and the second cable was cut also. A crack of gunfire echoed through the valley. He sprinted back to the tower, sliding into it with a crunching sound. The metalwork began to groan.

He hacked away at the tower with his Thorn. The dull, heavy bark of the metal rang out rhythmically into the night. The chorus of shrieking rose. Another shot was fired. The bullet pierced the shell a few yards from him. A nasaled grousing sounded high above him, possibly from the sniper.

It'll take too long.

He left the maul were it lay, stuck in the tower. Shimmering golden sand was pouring freely from it, bouncing and scattering as it hit the ground.

Krejcarek might kill him.

More likely one of the snipers.

He took in a deep breath of peppermint. "Everything has a price."

He took hold of the maul. He lit his fire. The maul burst forth into a flaming great sword, pushing against him as it sheered away the metal in its path. He switched his grip, tore it loose, and brought it full-circle to cleave deep into the opposite side of the tower. Another crack of gunfire. It kicked the air from his lungs. His knees buckled. He held onto his great sword, lifting himself, finding his footing again. He couldn't pull in a breath. The shot had come from a different tower. His Blackroot swallowed the bullet. With a growl he wrenched his sword through, nearly severing the tower. Then he strode around. He took one of the tower's girders in his gauntlet, and with a scream, pulled it down. The squeal and groan of crippled metal.

Silence.

The resounding clap and crash as it smashed to the ground. Dust and ash blossomed from the wreckage.

The Drekavacs' cries split the air. His body crumbled. He dropped his Thorn to cover his ears. The sound ripped through his body. His vision doubled. He felt another bullet pierce the ground beside him. He grabbed his great sword and stumbled away, toward the top of the shell. The shrieking in his exposed ear was a white-hot pain. His great sword became a dagger. He sheathed it, and covered his other ear as quickly as possible. He hurried along the iron arm, using it as cover.

His lungs burned. It felt as though they were filled with boiling water. His vision blurred. His head pulsed with pain. The peppermint began to turn, mingling with the tang of rotting lemons. Two gunshots rang out. One of them struck the iron arm. He ran.

The Drekavacs' shrieking lessened with the distance. He finally dropped his hands. The sound was still nauseating, scratching at the inside of his skull. A volley of gunfire erupted to his right. One of them grazed his bare leg. One ricocheted off his pauldron. The Blackroot raised his arm. He whimpered from the effort. A pavise shield of Blackroot bulged and tumified, crawling its way out of him, catching several bullets, drawing them into its chitinous mass. He hobbled forward, the pavise latched to his right arm, the iron wall to his left.

He couldn't see Krejcarek's dome yet.

Just like the chimney forest.

He let that go. More and more gunfire crackled around him. His Blackroot twisted, creeping out over him, weighing him down, and slowing his movements.

Another bullet struck his back. He staggered, but kept his footing. The Blackroot swallowed that lead too.

Three soldiers sprinted from the haze. His Blackroot thickened. He drew his Thorn.

Save it for him.

They're in my way.

He rammed the pavise into them as full speed. He returned his Thorn to his waistband. A hammer cracked his Blackroot. He staggering backwards. But his Blackroot knew where to strike. One by one, the soldiers were laid down and scattered across the shell.

Gunfire continued. He threw himself against the iron arm once more, the pavise pulled tight against his side. He trudged on.

The iron arms were drawing closer to each other. He could see a few of them now, their malignant fires blazing, all of them leading to the same place. But he couldn't see the dome yet.

Just like the chimney forest.

He pulled down his mask. "Krejcarek!" he cried out, coughing up a lung-full of putrid smoke.

More gunfire screamed as it struck the iron wall. A corner of the pavise shattered. He fell back against the wall. It was too heavy to carry.

"I'll finish cracking open your head, Krejcarek!" he roared spitefully into the night.

A hoard rushed screaming from the haze. He shouted back, pushing off the iron arm, lumbering at them. More bullets pierced his Blackroot. He tore a mace from his Blackroot with a roar. He swung it wildly, striking and crushing the soldiers that mobbed him. The pavise shattered. He slashed at them with the jagged remains. Someone was still firing. His sight dimmed. They kept coming. He stumbled over the bodies. He couldn't stop coughing. A shove to the back. A strike to the temple. He fell. They crushed him into the ground beneath their numbers. The Blackroot flexed, driving spikes up into their flesh and armor. The masses writhed and wriggled on top of him, clawing at his skirt, armor, and skin.

Just like the chimney forest.

A voice boomed over him. The hoard persisted. Gunfire. Screaming. Blood splattered on the young man's face and armor. The voice came once more. The hoard began to relent.

They fell away, crawled away, making space, dragging each other off him. They dragged away the dead and injured. The young man coughed violently, curling up on his side and holding his mouth. He pulled the mask back on, pressing it to his face with both hands. The faint relief of peppermint filled his burning mouth and nose. Tears continued streaming from blinded eyes.

The booming voice said something. They grabbed him by the arms and dragged him away. It took three of them.

They dragged him a long distance.

He told his Blackroot to wait,
even though it didn't want to.

The tops of his feet felt strange,
drawn across ridges of the tortoise shell.

He wasn't sure where they were taking him.
He hoped he knew.

His Thorn was missing.
He could feel it.

They were going to kill him.

Everything has a price.

He hadn't heard it before,
but the soldiers were coughing.
One of them stopped to retched.

They threw him to the ground. His claws raked over the oily, dirty shell. The Drekavac had fallen silent. Or at least their cries were not railing against his skull anymore. The termite soldiers grumbled and chittered among themselves. There were fat flakes of white ash around him.

A voice was coughing at a distance in front of him. The booming voice from before. He could barely see, but he looked up to watch the white ash fall like snow, luminous flecks of fluttering white against a shapeless black sky, flitting and swaying in the fitful air, landing silently on the tortoise shell, the iron arms that flanked him, and the iron dome before him.

The iron dome was a giant structure made of three domes, one inside the other, connected by braces. It made him think of a chokecherry bush for some reason. Barbed spikes jutted from every surface, and the only way into the dome was through a very narrow hallway of more spiked iron rod. Black banners were raised on every surface. On top of the iron arms, on top of the dome, and flanking the hallway. They flapped fitfully in the desolate wind. The young man had been thrown down in front of that hallway.

At the center of the dome, seated on a crudely-made wooden throne, on a crudely-made wooden platform, lounged a fat, proud, and spiteful General Krejcarek. The young man had to squint to see him at all. The general looked different than before. The metal staples that held his split head together. The ornate, spiked pauldron on his left shoulder. His faithful Whitworth was laid across his lap. Sashes of medals and trinkets were draped over his round chest. And he held a tall, ornate hammer in his hand, standing upright next to his throne. An even larger banner with its white hash-mark symbol stood behind the general's throne. Many weapons were strewn about his platform like treasure.

But he was a suffering creature. His spiky, blood-red exoskeleton was crusted in oily film and blackened filth, and the white ash was falling on him as well, a dusting on his head, shoulders, and the tops of his sarouel pants. His black, beady eyes were glistening, weeping, drawing clean lines down the cracks of his face and into his compulsive, ravenously chewing mandibles. His chest rose and fell with much effort, and his breath was labored. He was constantly clearing his throat.

"'Just as long as she dies with me'," the young man could barely get the words out before he wheezed, a chuckle mixed with coughing. The chimney forest seemed like a distant memory in that moment.

"I promised you," Krejcarek called out. "Did I not, you stupid, simple boy? You cannot stop me. Even your clever little witch couldn't touch me—what makes you think you could do any better?"

Let it go.

The young man tried to stand. A bullet ripped into his thigh. He cried out in agony, collapsing to the ground.

Make him suffer.

Krejcarek threw away the discharged Whitworth and stood, leaning on his ornate hammer. "Did I tell you to stand? Did I give you permission? You are in The King's way, heretic!" He shook his hammer. "And you will bear witness to my King's will." Then he turned, stifling a fit of coughing with his forearm.

> *He's gonna kill you.*
> *Let it go.*

Blackroot swarmed around the wound, binding it tightly. But there was something different about it. Maybe the bullet.

The young man was humming one of Monkey's silly songs, his eyes shut tight, his forehead pressed against the ground. He couldn't drown out his thoughts.

He wanted to fight.

He wanted to run away.

It didn't matter what he wanted.

> *Let it go.*
> *He underestimates you.*

Cold sweat broke out on his face as the pain began to swell, radiating through his whole body. He winced, rolling onto his side, propping himself up with an elbow.

"That it? That's your big speech?" He pulled down his mask and looked up at one of the soldiers beside him. It glanced back at him in misery. "I just thought there'd be more." He gestured to the General, "—I would've done more."

"You want more?" Krejcarek bellowed. He pulled the young man's Thorn from the back of his belt. It wasn't bleeding sand. The young man leaned forward.

Krejcarek threw away his hammer and lumbered up to the spikes of his dome, his mandibles frothing.

"Is this yours?" he displayed the dagger. "It's mine." He beat the fist that held that dagger against his chest.

"Your valley? Mine." He struck himself even harder, the medals on his sashes chiming in chorus.

"Your witch? Mine!"

The young man flicked his wrist as Krejcarek struck the final time.

The general collapsed forward, his arms swinging, his boots sliding and kicking behind him. But he didn't hit the ground. The young man's Thorn was now a spear. It was planted deep in the ground, and pierced clean through Krejcarek's skull.

The Blackroot released all of its bullets in a volley of hissing sounds. The soldiers that surrounded him fell. Those that could, screeched, writhed, or crawled away.

He rolled onto his back. "Now, my love, NOW!!!" The young man cried as loudly as his lungs could suffer. But he hadn't needed to.

A tower lit up the sky. A singular blade of lightning smote it. Then another tower fell. And then another. A handful of soldiers came for him. He struck down some. Others fled when they saw Krejcarek. One was dragged away into the night by black dogs. He could hear the fear and despair in the cries that surrounded him, horrific noises from beyond the black haze, the despair of the fallen and the fearful sounding in every direction. The blinding fury of lightning struck again and again, points of ruthless white in the blackness of night, until all nine towers were accounted for.

He had to sit down. He limped to one of the iron arms and slid to the filthy ground next to it. His leg hurt. It was a coldness. A stinging dullness. He pulled up his skirt. The Blackroot was still wrapping the bullet wound.

The chitinous rootwork crept in circles. The smallest, scarlet roots kept reaching, shifting, weaving back into itself, over and over again. Something was wrong.

He was still seated when the witch approached. She was younger than before, her skin painted artfully in blood and white ash, her short hair slicked back. A black mask covered her nose and mouth. Her utility belt was missing. His heart sank. In her hand was a sniper rifle, gripped by the barrel, swinging from her hip. It was scorched, bent, and chipped. She had clearly been using it as a club. It was always nice to look at her.

He rose clumsily to meet her. She tossed away her weapon, ran her fingers along the inside of her mask, reset it, and then drew those fingers along the inside of his mask. The flavor of peppermint returned when she reset his mask over his nose.

"You," she began as she did her work, "Are a dangerous creature." The wrinkles from a smile could be seen around her clouded, watering eyes. It accented her tear-shaped scar.

He took longer than he wanted to come up with a reply. "I'm sure you say that to all the ... creatures."

The two entered the dome, stepping sideways through the spike-lined hallway. He felt the tip of a spike scratch against this Blackroot, a dull, thick sound to a shallow cut.

Then they were standing before the general. He was still alive. White blood and steaming venom dribbled and oozed out of every orifice. The spear had pierced through the top of his head next to the staples, cracking open a new, wider wound. His eyes were bulging, still leaking tears in pulses which splashed down his cheeks. One of his hands was loosely gripping the spear. The opposite knee was twitching, jerking hard to the side every once in a while. His shimmering eyes seemed to follow them. His mandibles gyrated slowly, as though he might be trying to say something. The young man almost felt sorry for him.

"Tiger needs us," he said, unable to find a better way to say what they both knew all too well.

The witch turned to him, placing her hand on his scar. "I need a moment."

He didn't need to know her thoughts to understand her.

The young man turned to Krejcarek. "She's all yours," he said, and left the dome.

He didn't look back. He couldn't distinguish what she was saying. The other voice must've been the general, quiet, simpering, choking, slurred and helpless. Her voice rose, the calls of a mother-warrior. Krejcarek must have tried to answer, his slovenly, desperate tones rising with hers, almost like choking, almost like crying. A high pitched, gasping whine. The iron dome lit with electricity from the inside, a blinding, deafening crash that hammered the metal over and over again. The young man couldn't dare look back. He braced himself, careful of his bad leg, and reminding himself to not touch the iron arms. He was uncertain whether it was the pealing of thunder strikes, the cry of the witch, or the pleas of the General, but a horrific sound rode upon the relentless devastation. It didn't stop until the final thunder clap boomed, echoing, fading, dancing off the darkened valley walls.

Once all had quieted, the young man turned around. A bountiful, gossamer-white vapor had enveloped the iron dome. The witch eventually shuffled from the vapor. She carried his Thorn. In her other hand was a pike; Krejcarek's head was skewered on the end of it. He limped to her. She was much older again, with streaks of frangible white hair. Her mask was missing.

Her skin was steaming, her dress even more torn, with great stripes of it singed with stripes of shock-white. She met the young man, coming to a stop before him. Her face was weathered, with patches of still-smoldering burns. And yet she was calm. She handed his Thorn to him and nodded. "I feel better now."

4

The two returned the way they had come. The wolf carried him. It was not a discussion he could win. She tore along the uneven valley wall, navigating the swaths of loose soil and scree, and carving between the burning trees, grass, and bushes. Everything that wasn't on fire was coated with a dense covering of dark ash. The storm of white flakes was falling fast and thick now, making it even more difficult to see through the haze. They flew by the rows upon rows of soldiers. It seemed as though there were more of them somehow. He held Krejcarek's pike high, screaming at the hoards as they raced past.

At last they could see the dark shape of the grove ahead. It didn't appear to be on fire at that distance. The army seemed to be pressed against it, somehow still held at bay. They couldn't see Tiger's fire. She gained more speed. They could sode a group of giants near the right edge of the valley, four or five of them crowded together, knocking against each other, working on something. Everything was shrouded. Everything was muddled. He leaned forward, squinting. A striped tail whipped up above the giants' heads.

He dropped Krejcarek's head and pike. She dug deep, sprinting even faster.

He could see more clearly as they approached. The giants held their clubs and swords and spears high, stabbing and swinging downward with a savage strength. Goblin and termite soldiers crawled on the giants' shoulders and backs, crammed between their legs, scuttling and wriggling over each other.

They were too far away.

An orange blur galloped down the side of the valley. Monkey leaped, throwing himself into the giants. He tackled one, knocking down another. Soldiers swarmed Monkey, clawing and pouring over each other to get to him. Gunfire and flailing weapons. The giant was thrashing him, throwing its fists wildly.

I'll get Monkey.

The young man barely finished the thought before he was flying over the melee of helmets and spear tips. His Thorn was a double-bladed battleaxe clad in Blackroot. He struck the giant at full speed, driving the ax deep into its back. The giant staggered off of Monkey, rising urgently, gasping, scattering soldiers in its breathless fervor. The Blackroot wormed deeper. He worked the ax in for good measure. Then he launched himself off the giant, kicking it into the mud, pulling free his Thorn in the process. A sickening crack.

He landed on his bad leg. He fell, hitting the mud, sliding to a stop. Shooting pains. He clutched his thigh. There was no time. He dragged himself to his feet and limped toward Monkey. One of the blades of the ax had broken off in the giant. He couldn't grow it back.

He hacked away at the soldiers as the came, throwing them aside and cleaving limbs. A Blackroot mace was in his other hand. He split flesh and shattered bone as he carved out a circle around Monkey. He limped when he could. He screamed when he had to. A spear or gunshot would sometimes splinter his Blackroot, knocking him back, but a new plate always grew in its place.

Golden sand was rising all around him. He didn't ignite his fire so he wouldn't burn Monkey. He could only catch glimpses of his old friend in the mania. Monkey was stirring, but there was so much blood, and many spears were stuck in his body. The young man put down another soldier, plunging his ax deep into the termite's neck. He jerked it free with an agonizing kick to the chest. Another sickening crack.

He fell backward into the mud. The clouds of golden sands dropped in a single breath. The second blade had broken off. The shattered ruby lay scattered beside him. He tried to sit up. His leg twitched with shooting pains. He looked to his guardian.

Monkey lay sprawled out next to him on the bloody, sandy, mud-smeared ground. His body had been devestated, his flesh and fur singed and torn, riddled with tall spears and gaping bullet wounds. He was little more than wandering, fearful eyes and a battered face, wild with blinding pain.

His wolf was beside him, the malignant air surging with electricity. "We have this. Go."

The staff of the battleaxe was crumbling to dust in his hand.

Tiger was alive again, a roaming tempest of purple flame consuming the army. The giants had arrived.

She hadn't moved. "Are you alright?"

Tiger needs her.

"I got this!" he gasped. "I got it."

She hesitated. A worried look in her eye. Then she bolted away.

The young man dragged Monkey toward the grove. The spikes on his Blackroot pierced his guardian's arm. He fell more than once. Monkey was trying to say something but the young man couldn't understand it. They left a wide and wet trail of blood.

The wolf was threshing the front line. A few straggling soldiers broke through. Sometimes he had to drop Monkey's arm and beat them back with his Blackroot.

Monkey was stuck with two more spears.

The young man was moaning, shuddering as he dragged his dear friend's limp body. Every muscle was hollow, sapped of strength. He could barely lean on his bad leg.

A rifleman shot Monkey in the belly; he was lanced by lightning.

Tiger and the wolf devastated the army, slaughtering wave after bloody wave. Droves of black dogs were harvesting the fallen soldiers. He wondered why they weren't coming for Monkey.

The curtains of willow branches draped over his back as he pulled Monkey into the shadow of the grove.

~

With much effort, the young man laid Monkey down against a fallen log. The clearing was robed in heavy shadows. Wide ribbons of smoke drifted lazily through the air. The two towering willows which made the archway stood watch over them. The relentless sounds of war were a distant muttering through the gently swaying curtain of branches.

The young man was kneeling next to Monkey. His hand was on his guardian's chest, feeling the shallow, uneven breaths he could pull. His lady had taught him enough about war injuries to lose hope. Bullets tear open vital organs. Sometimes removing a blade or bullet can be more damaging then letting it be. Some things can't be healed.

He said Python's name many times, a muttering, a question, a withered sigh. Nothing happened. He filled his lungs and cried out for Python, a long and desperate scream.

Nothing.

He laid his head gently into Monkey's matted, muddied fur, sobbing.

Monkey mumbled, "You're going to make this weird, aren't you?"

He jerked upright, stammering out the words, "My Thorn. I found it. But it's broken. I—I can't fix this."

He cried out for Python again.

Monkey winced at the volume of his voice, laying his great hand gently on the young man's shoulder. "No, no. Ah, you couldn't heal me anyway. I'm not magic like you or Tiger, or even your lady. It doesn't work that way. The only magic I have is my deeply, awe-inspiring good looks. They fear how much they love me, really."

But the young man was already up, stumbling toward the curtain of branches. "I'll be right back."

"Your lady can't heal me," Monkey called out, using more strength than he had. " … Honestly, I'm not sure why you keep her around. Only two kids … "

The young man was frozen at the curtain of willow branches, his armored fists pressed against the sides of his head. "Why? WHY!!!" he cried, turning on Monkey. "Why are you doing this? You're bleeding—you are dying. And they are fighting for our lives out there!"

"And you should be out there too." Monkey blinked his bleary eyes, unable to find a comfortable position.

"I'm not going to leave you."

Monkey sighed. "So what's the game, little Sprout? Are you going to rub my feet? Because you should let me know if that's an option. No pressure, I'm just curious."

He hobble back to Monkey, awkwardly falling to his knees, begging, "I don't know. I don't. I can't … "

Monkey gripped the back of his neck, trembling, but tenderly. He muffled a cough. "Tell me a story. And then let me go."

He shook his head, his shoulders hunched, his body lifeless.

Monkey smiled dimly. "I've got a strange feeling you're gonna do what the dying monkey asks."

He took hold of his dear friend's arm. It was all the assent he could muster.

"Who did this?" Monkey asked, nodding to the sounds beyond the grove.

"Krejcarek."

He made a noise of disapproval. "I was curious. No way to know for sure … Wow, what a petty turd."

"Yeah, he's one immaculate tool."

"Hey there, let's just call him a "standard tool". That thing doesn't deserve more than a two-syllable descriptor … You got him?"

The young man nodded. "Yeah, I got him."

"Big man," he said with a weary grin.

"My lady cooked him with lightning."

Monkey stared into the middle-distance. He tilted his head. "I can't think of a response to that."

The young man laughed hard at that—deep, from his belly—but it was immediately choked back with sobbing.

Monkey brushed aside his hair. "Tough crowd."

"I'm sorry, I just—"

"And you were doing so good there. I genuinely thought you would make it through a whole conversation without apologizing." Monkey doubled up, seizing, and turned away coughing blood and spittle. It took a long time. When he laid back again he was shivering, shifting and trembling from exhaustion.

The young man had no words, he looked helplessly to his guardian.

Monkey pressed on, his voice like gravel. "Do you want to know the final punchline? You'll like it. It's a good one: people do what they want. No matter what they say, no matter how they explain them selves, it's always the same. So when I'm gone, if you stay sad—living in regret, or get mean, or give up, or run away—you can't pin that on me. Because you're only doing that for yourself. Now ask me what I want for you."

He squeezed Monkey's arm with both hands. "What do you want?"

"I want you to forgive, and let people forgive you. I want you to be willing to laugh at your mistakes ..." He fumbled about, searching for the young man's hands. The young man met him. Monkey laid the broken pieces of the ruby in his palms. He nodded when he felt them land, pushing them toward the young man. "I want you to be whole again."

The young man gripped them tightly. The crunch of the pieces being pressed together. "It—it's broken. It doesn't work anymore. I don't know how."

Monkey grin was wide and calm. "No, it's not. Yes, it does. And yes, you do. I bet my life on it."

The young man jumped as Python emerged from the underbrush. "I am here," she said.

"He's dying," he said, standing, limping back, the ruby pieces in his grip. "Please, do something."

Python slowly, gently slid under him, coiling up around Monkey, cradling him, lifting him, supporting his neck and legs. "I am here, my sweet, silly old friend."

Monkey let out a sigh of relief and discomfort as she methodically came to rest beneath him. "Hey there, gorgeous. Someone said something about a foot rub earlier." He looked to the young man with pride and said, "You're going to be late to the dance."

"Okay," was all he could say.

"Are you going to do what I asked?"

The young man choked back a sob. "I'll try."

"That's my boy."

The young man, hopeless and weary, looked down at the broken pieces of ruby in his hands. He took them, one by one, and placed them back into his stomach, from where they were taken, just below his rib cage. There was nothing magical about it. Many times he thought he was going to pass out, or retch. But Monkey and Python were watching. So he stood his ground, bent his knees, dug his toes in, and finished what he had started.

When it was all done he didn't feel any different. Tired, for certain. But he was no better than he was before. And that was okay. The world seemed somehow more nuanced. The air, more dense. The colors, more detailed. The ground, heavier as it held up his feet. He took a deep breath.

"Oh," he said, looking again.

It was like waking up for the first time. More radiant, more alive, more ordinary, and more predictable than he had ever seen before. He searched the clearing with a lovely, pensive, disappointing wonder. But only for a moment.

He turned to Python. "My children?"

"Safe and sound," she said.

"I love you both. I love you." He turned, limping toward the curtain of willow branches. His Blackroot flexed and wove around him, ratcheting down his shoulders, arms, and through his spine. It threaded deep into his wounded leg, cinching and binding. An array of curved blades sprouted from his pauldrons and gauntlets. But he had chosen every one of their places and forms. Two weapons twisted and burst forth, growing from the wrists of his clawed gauntlets, a short sword and a war hammer. He lit his fire, and a rush of pale, gilded sand scattered, swarming, rising in the air, turning about him, awash in the churning flames. Wildflowers burst into bloom at his feet, and each footstep called sprouts of wildflowers to blossom in his wake. He leaned in, striding, testing out his bad leg. One by one, the curtains of willow branches parted before him, and he jogged out into the thunderous bedlam that lay beyond.

~

It took three days and two nights to finish the war.

He found the pike with Krejcarek's head and fixed it in
the ground near the entrance to the grove. Some of the
soldiers ran in fear when they saw it. A few fought even
harder at the sight. Some didn't react at all; they had
never known the face of their general.

They were able to convince the Tarasque to retreat,
to shuffle backward out of the valley,
and wander off to wherever it might chose to roam.

They buried Monkey on the third evening,
near the great willow.

From then on it was called the Valley of the Dead,
or Black Dog Valley.
Many books after this call it Dog Valley.

The young man's left leg was crippled.
He refused his lady's offers to try and heal him.
He said he'd rather have the days with her.
He walked with a limp the rest of his life.

The young witch became more solitary,
especially as the children grew into adolescence.
She began leaving on long trips,
and her gaze was often drawn towards the horizon.

Tiger lost one of his eyes in the battle.
Having burned countless years of his life,
he was never the same after the war.

Python did as she had always done.
But she spoke less.

Black dogs feasted on the valley for the next seasons,
picking clean the dead,
leaving weapons and machinery behind to rust.
Thieves and robbers
scavenged the valley for years to come.
They almost never disturbed the grove.
Certain stories had spread.

The stench of death and decay
lingered in the valley for a whole year.

The flowers came back much sooner.

~

THORN

~

Book II

of

The Grove Trilogy

SKETCH
GALLERY

SPROUT

THORN

BLACKROOT

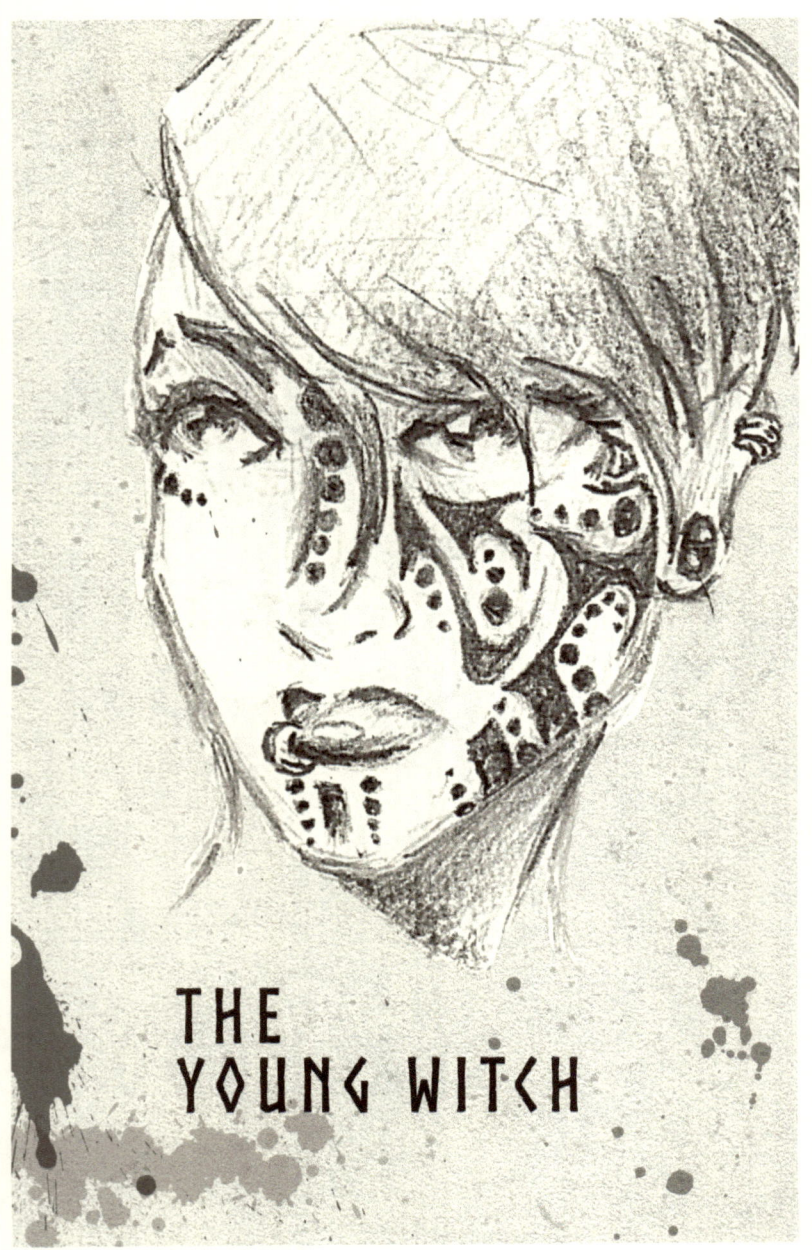

THE
YOUNG WITCH

CLOTH
GAUNTLET
AND
JEWELRY

Ian Abdo

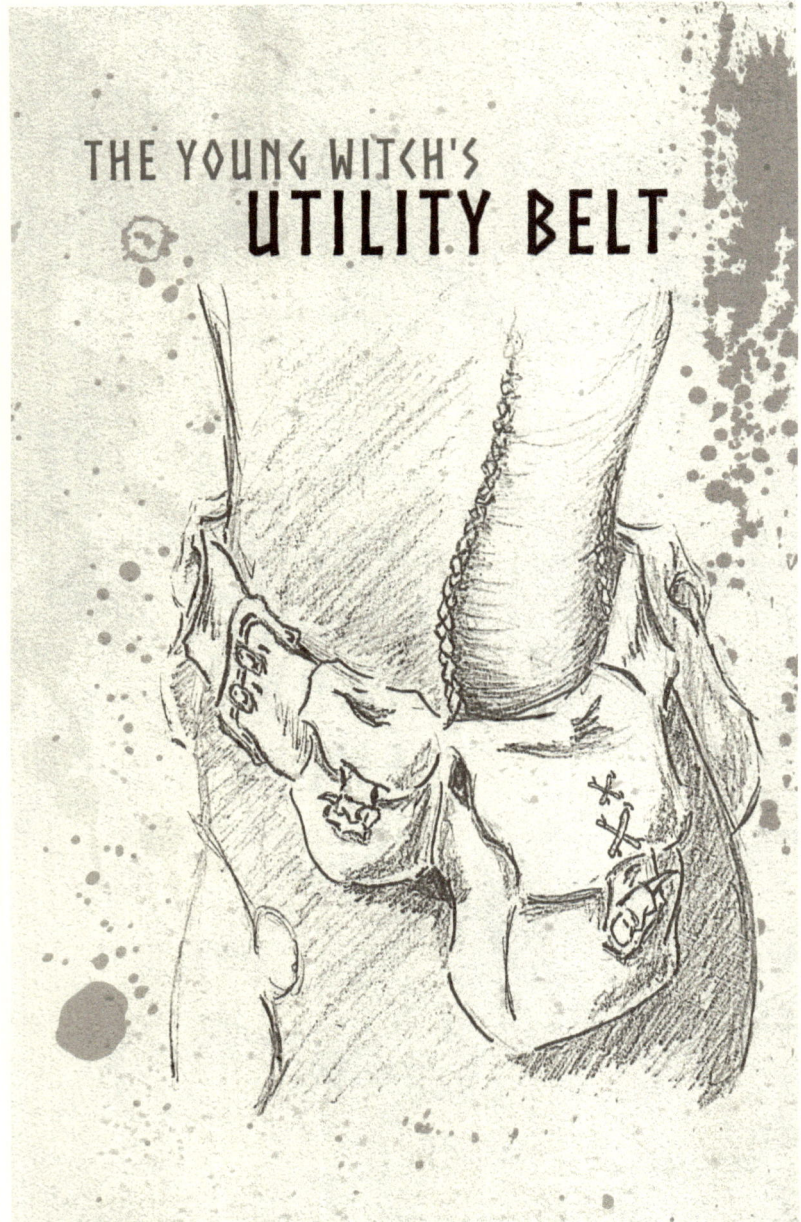

THE YOUNG WITCH'S
UTILITY BELT

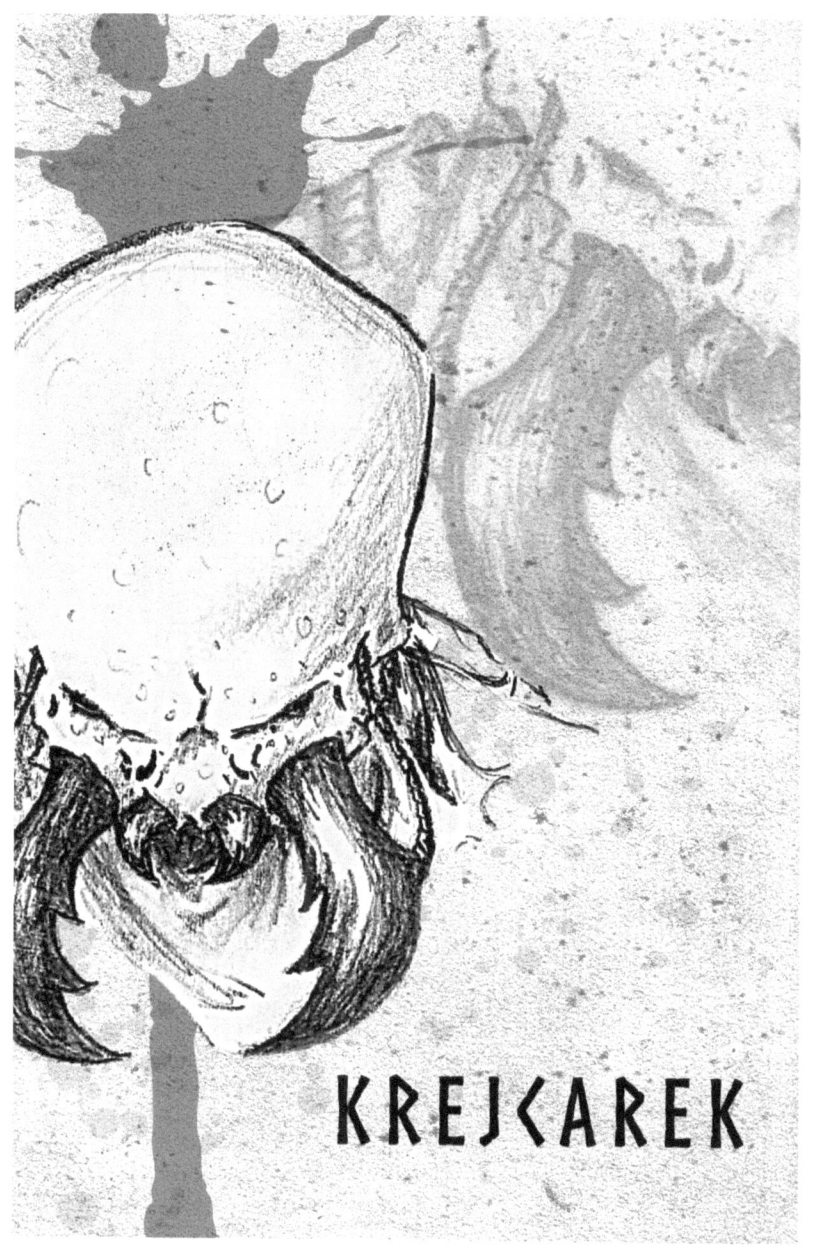

SIGIL
OF THE
DESERT
KING,
ATTICE

BESTIARY

~

We're all beasts in here.

—Lady Toolis,
of the Arcane Consortium of Lavanya

Lavanya

Born from the tears of the Dragon Armastus, the Lavanya are a wild and trackless women who wander the pages of Lark. Born from different outpourings, hatched long after Armastus had shed them from her cheeks, the far-cast orphanhood eventually discovered each other, forming bonds, contentions, sisterhoods, arch-rivalries, and sects, thus embracing the profuse and diverse roles each was compelled to satisfy in the world; in passion, in fellowship, in slavery, or governance.

Without unique characteristics to mark each sub-species—besides the vague and yet ubiquitous pixie-like attributes—the four sects are most easily distinguished by their respective matriarchal textile/material, which, interestingly enough, they are instinctively loathed to abandon.*

Steer clear of these women. For the slightest glance, the smallest of words, the lightest touch, could eviscerate as easily as it emancipates.

Ymrosch

"Middling Son," is the only description reliably identified in association with this Jotnar. It is uncertain whether this is a title of familial station or of character.

What we do know is that he was, indeed, a child of Ymir, the primeval being from whom the very pages of Lark were manufactured.

Ymrosch is rarely ever mentioned in the First Texts —and even more rarely by name. It is hypothesized that his virtual absence is a result of his rejection from the tribe long before their inevitable and tragic extermination.

The only further documentation of this Jotnar comes from the admittedly spartan texts of the 'lost tribes' of Rough Drafts.* While hotly contested, the two presiding theories suggest that Ymrosch was either the author of the lost tribe's demise, or the impotent witness to their downfall.

The Goatmen

The standing army of the Spiteful King—so named Jonnakas, the Twelve-Horned Conqueror, the Vexing Warlord of Crescent Bay—the Goatmen are his unstoppable force, a tireless infantry known for their merciless will and unquenchable blood-lust.

But how much is truly known of these far-flung, nautical warriors? Should we, nestled in our spiral towers, safe within the Red Queen's stalwart and secure domain, fat and thoroughly at ease on our cushioned pedestals, be so swift to pronounce these people as "savage"? Is it not we, who flippantly condemn a people we know so little of, we who garner coin for the elaborate and surgical fables we fabricate like an unflagging flood of mind-numbing fodder, be branded as the derogatory lot?* But such things are not for this Archivist to decree.

Wardens of the Edge of the World, they are known to capture and subdue lesser Dragons for use in battle, to torture and execute prisoners for sport, and employ all manor of alchemical warcraft. Girded by innumerable forms of military hardware, the Goatmen are, empirically, without equal.*

Black Dogs

Origin, unknown.
Lifespan, unknown.
Functionality within the ecosystem, unquantifiable.

All information concerning this species is purely speculative. Any fanatical attribution of the Author's hand in the creation of this species has become, thankfully, entirely irrelevant.

A broadly-acknowledged observation is that these beasts gather, with some sort of supernatural awareness, before a world-altering event. This evidence is circumstantial at best.*

Aberrations on the species have been well-documented, anecdotally. This Archivist is, however, not at liberty to speak of such, "Coincidences".

Minotaurs

The tales surrounding this species are dubious.* Many have rallied to confirm the progenitor of the race as a desperate survivor of a carnal and unscrupulous transaction between a Dragon and an eccentric landowner. Details have been lost in the countless re-tellings.*

Any information that could be extracted is empirically slanderous, if not entirely salacious. This Archivist finds it unorthodox that such a vulgar beast, employed by lord and cretin alike, would require acknowledgment in this Bestiary. Perish the thought a scribe might be remunerated according to cumulated pages transcribed.

Perhaps the only noteworthy characteristic of the Minotaur is its arbitrary capacity to manifest supernatural abilities, perhaps due to its … exotic genealogy. This includes but is not limited to: ostio-genesis, laceration transmission, and the condition colloquially known as "Iron blood".

Ian Abdo

Tarasque

Even more tragic than the Minotaur, the Tarasque has been maligned by the masses for far too long. Considered a minor pest by the majority of paupers, the pre-pubescent Tarasque has been the trapped and tortured animal "righteously exorcised" from many an ignorant farmer's tale.* The fully grown beast is not so easily disposed.

Consider an exotic creature as tall as a mountain, as wide as a valley, unperturbed by the petulant, unceasing requirements of this inane, artificial, and quarrelsome modern life. One might find oneself envious, if such a thing was permitted.

Nevertheless, these mature beasts exist in an unrivaled echelon. Every footstep is as an earthquake. Their daily diet is the equivalent foliage of a small country, if one could imagine. Though many an archivist has claimed that this is a land animal, the reports of a Tarasque—even great packs no less—sailing in deep waters cannot be so easily discounted.

Truly, to sent one's eyes on such an Elder Beast would be the finest moment of one's miserly existence.

Drekavac

What can be said of such a virulent pest? The Drekavac is, without peer, the most pervasive and stubborn of vermin. They most often appear as children, though their skin has all but decayed. Their hair and nails grow to repulsive lengths.

Avoid these creatures at all cost. For should you stumble upon even a single Drekavac, it could be your undoing. Capable of pouncing from great distances, they are known to grip flesh and cloth and hair with an unnatural, unyielding strength. Their piercing cries are known to cause madness, rampant homicide, blindness, deafness, unflagging insanity, and in the most unfortunate of cases, death.

Occupying castle and cottage alike, this insidious creature can appear without wont or warning, forcing entire populations to evacuate in a single night.

The Red Queen herself has assured the people of Lark that, "Top alchemists are working on it. Fixing as quick as quick can be. Consider it sorted."

There is currently no cure for such beasts.

Ian Abdo

Hagen

A most elusive beast, the Hagen have a convoluted and circuitous history. Some staunchly propose that the Hagen adopted their name only after many pages of heinous and harrowing acts had been attributed to this cadre of assassins.*

Known for having only one eye, it is unclear whether this is an evolutionary trait, or a stringent rite of passage.* Despite this, they are without question hailed as a race of exacting, extraordinary marksman.

But the historical accusations are innumerable, and paint a vivid picture for us to extrapolate an articulate—and quite graphic—understanding of this race; patricidal, fratricidal, filicidal, nepoticidal, or any other -cidal one might be able to worm from one's mind; their devious and underhanded nature is obvious, bringing to question the stability of their culture, and its potential endurance as a species.*

*Citation requested
*Impartial citation required
 in light of Archivist's termination.

ABOUT THE AUTHOR

Ian Abdo is like a cat. Imagine all the grace and intractability of that animal and you will understand him. Ian loves storytelling, meditation, a fine whiskey, and good Metal. He resides in the Rogue Valley, OR, with his brilliant family, where he bakes sweets and scribbles words. *Thorn* is his second published work.

Feel free to visit our website,
www.ianabdo.com

Epilogue

~

The old man sat on the broken stone dais next to the old and gnarled willow. His long and scraggly beard was stained with wine. His dark robes were threadbare and filthy. He cradled his clay cup of hearty wine against the side of his belly. He was clapping his good knee to a rambling tune that he was humming. It was midday, and the half-circle of willows lay still and empty, heavy shadow cut by streams of blazing sunlight.

The old man had heard the commotion, the rustling of bushes and the intermittent, frantic exclamations that accompanied these uninvited guests. He had been half-listening to the approaching intrusion as he kept to his tune, and his wine, until a goblin was thrown down in the hard light at the center of the circle. It was badly beaten, with only a loin cloth to cover its misshapen, hairy body. It cowered and clung to itself in the chill of fear and discombobulation.

The old man craned his neck, looking to the bold and broad cloaked figure that had brought the goblin, still hidden in shadow. He squinted, a little from the light, a little more from the wine. The wide shoulders, the stiff, upright posture, the sweeping white hair and beard. He wasn't wearing his regal armor, but there was no mistaking a king.

"Hail, Uncle Perdue! My stars, you haven't aged a day. Maybe a year? Hard to tell from here, honestly …" He heaved himself upright as he downed a swig from his cup and then began searching about where he was seated. "I have wine, somewhere."

"No thank you, I won't waste your time." Perdue turned to the goblin. "Speak. Tell him what you told me."

The goblin flinched at the sound of Perdue's voice. It swallowed loudly as it ran its long fingers through the wild, unkempt grass. A nasal voice came from his crooked mouth: "He moves. Like a shadow across the land, he is. And those in his wake are without number, yes, yes." The goblin turned its watery eyes upon the old man. "A storm is coming."

"Hey, HEY!" the old man jumped lamely to his feet. He turned to Perdue and threw his arms in the air. "What are you doing? Why would you bring this into my house?" He cast a look of exasperation at you before continuing, "I mean, sure, we've all dabbled in the pronoun game, but come on. 'A storm is coming'? Really?" He was bent over now, searching more thoroughly for the wine as he mumbled, "Is the rose of rage ready to be pruned? … Soon the corn of vengeance shall be shucked?"

"SPROUT!!!" Perdue boomed.

The old man turned on him, "I haven't seen you in pa —*years* and now you show up with this?" he gestured to the pathetic and baffled creature in the light.

Perdue, fuming, stormed up to the goblin, casting his long shadow, his gloved hand raised as a threat. "Say his name, creature!"

The goblin shrank even lower, groveling. "The King!" it shrieked. "The King who never Dies!"

Perdue looked on the old man gravely. "Attice rides for your grove, little Sprout."

It took a moment for the news to sink in. Then the old man shrugged drunkenly; he almost laughed. "So? The kids are gone, left years ago. It's just me."

Perdue walked towards him. "All things die in his presence. All things rot in his shadow."

"You've been spending too much time with our little poet over there."

"Sprout," Perdue laid a heavy hand on the old man's shoulder. "Everything in this grove will die."

The old man met his eye with a glassy stare. "At least we won't lose anything important."

Perdue searched his face. His mustache twitched. He twisted about, his cloak sweeping behind him. "Useless," he muttered under his breath as he grasped the goblin by the scruff of his neck and strode out of the half-circle of willows.

"At least tell me what I'm looking at here," the old man called after him. "Do I have time for another skin of wine? Or is this more like a half-skin kind of scenario?"

"He arrives in three days!" Perdue bellowed back.

He frowned and nodded to himself.

The circle fell silent again.

He tilted his head, noticed a little wine left in his cup and lifted it to his lips. But he stopped short, hurled the cup, shattering it against the stones. The old man had liked that cup. He put his hands on his hips, hung his head, and sighed.

"I'm sorry you had to see that," he finally murmured. "No one likes a tired metaphor."